PRAISE F

"A winning lottery ticket, a haunted California mansion, and raging wildfires provide the tense and atmospheric backdrop for Wendy Corsi Staub's riveting and engrossing new thriller. I devoured this novel about the price of friendship and the things we'll do for love and money in one breathless sitting. Rocket-paced and full of unexpected twists, *Windfall* is a knockout! A summer must-read!"

**—LISA UNGER, *NEW YORK TIMES* BESTSELLING AUTHOR
OF *SECLUDED CABIN SLEEPS SIX***

"I couldn't turn the pages of *Windfall* fast enough in this twisty thriller that has it all—three friends who wrongly assumed they knew each other's secrets, a life-changing lottery ticket that could change their complicated lives for better (or worse), all in a Gothic setting on deadly cliffs shrouded by smoke from California wildfires. Nail-biting, tense, and rich—in more ways than one!"

—SARAH STROHMEYER, BESTSELLING AUTHOR OF *WE LOVE TO ENTERTAIN*

"What's scarier than a small slip of paper holding a billion-dollar lottery win to be split between three old friends? Add in a haunted mansion on a Pacific cliff surrounded by California wildfires, no phone or internet service, and you'll get a scream in the night and someone going missing. This is not just a perfect table setting of mystery elements, it's also a complex story of three women's lives, old college friends who find themselves lost in midlife, wondering what happened to all their youthful dreams and desires. Wendy Corsi Staub is at with her best with *Windfall*, keeping the reader on edge to find out who really wins it all in life and whose luck has run out."

"A tense and moving exploration of women's friendships and lives. Reading *Windfall* is like winning the lottery of suspense writing!"

"When money and old secrets collide, someone has to pay. It all comes due at Windfall. Compelling, atmospheric, and deliciously twisted. Suspense at its finest."

WINDFALL

Also by Wendy Corsi Staub

STANDALONE NOVELS
The Other Family

THE FOUNDLINGS SERIES
Little Girl Lost
Dead Silence
The Butcher's Daughter

MUNDY'S LANDING SERIES
Blood Red
Blue Moon
Bone White

SOCIAL MEDIA THRILLERS
The Black Widow
The Perfect Stranger
The Good Sister

NIGHTWATCHER TRILOGY
Nightwatcher
Sleepwalker
Shadowkiller

LIVE TO TELL TRILOGY
Live to Tell
Scared to Death
Hell to Pay

WINDFALL

A NOVEL OF SUSPENSE

WENDY CORSI STAUB

WM

An Imprint of HarperCollinsPublishers

WINDFALL. Copyright © 2023 by Wendy Corsi Staub. All rights reserved. Printed in the United States of America. No part of this book may be used or reproduced in any manner whatsoever without written permission except in the case of brief quotations embodied in critical articles and reviews. For information, address HarperCollins Publishers, 195 Broadway, New York, NY 10007.

HarperCollins books may be purchased for educational, business, or sales promotional use. For information, please email the Special Markets Department at SPsales@harpercollins.com.

FIRST EDITION

Designed by Renata De Oliveira

Library of Congress Cataloging-in-Publication Data has been applied for.

ISBN 978-0-06-323531-1

23 24 25 26 27 LBC 5 4 3 2 1

FOR BRYCE BERG,
who is kindness and positive energy, love and light.

And, as always, for Brody, Morgan, and Mark, with love.

*With gratitude to Lucia Macro, Liate Stehlik,
Asanté Simons, Amy Halperin, Gina Macedo, and the rest
of the team at HarperCollins/William Morrow;
to Laura Blake Peterson, James T. Farrell, and
Holly Frederick and the team at Curtis Brown, Ltd.;
to Alison Gaylin for the early read and vote of confidence;
to my Petty Pals, Friday Night Girls, and Sunrise Sisters
for lending an ear and shoulder; to the Californians, Tony
Gatto, and Laurie Corsi; to my family, especially Morgan
Staub, who so patiently listened, read multiple drafts, and
helped me work out many a plot point.*

Money often costs too much.

—RALPH WALDO EMERSON

Hello, and welcome to a brand-new season of *Disappearing Acts*. I'm host Riley Robertson, former investigative reporter, current podcaster, and perennial snoop!

This season, we're going to explore Hollywood's most intriguing mystery: *Whatever Happened to Chantal Charbonneau?*

The beautiful brunette was an A-list movie star with two Oscar nominations and fans all over the globe.

She was aloof and enigmatic, not one of those celebrities who relished fame, though she tolerated it and had even cultivated it when she was building a career.

Though she starred in some of the biggest box office hits of the 1990s, she became increasingly reclusive, which in turn fanned the flames of public interest in her personal life. By the time she disappeared in 2001, she was living in isolation at Windfall, her seaside estate north of Los Angeles.

The general consensus is that she's dead—that she either jumped, fell, or was pushed to her death and her body was swallowed by the sea. That makes sense, right?

Sure it does. And we're going to examine that theory.

We're also going to consider a far more intriguing one. What if she staged her disappearance in order to escape the spotlight and live out her days in obscurity?

WEDNESDAY

SHEA

May the dreams you hold dearest be those that come true.

Every night, for as long as Shea Daniels can remember, those are the last words she's heard before falling asleep.

Corey used to whisper them to her after they'd knelt for prayers, tucking in her quilt at the foot of the bed so that nothing scary could creep in with her while she was deep in slumber.

Now Shea whispers the words aloud to herself.

Corey, who'd loved and protected her and believed in dreams coming true, is long gone.

Corey, her parents, classmates, roommates, neighbors . . . so many others who were a part of her former life, have disappeared.

She's alone in the world now, has been alone for years; alone even when she's with a friend or colleague or her dogs. Alone even—no, especially—when a man shares her bed, creating a solitude more profound than being on her own in the dark.

There hasn't been a man in months now. Not since December. But when there was, she'd wait until he'd drifted off before she got up to tuck in the quilt so that nothing could creep in. Then she'd slip back between the sheets, turn toward the wall, and whisper, *May the dreams you hold dearest be those that come true.*

It doesn't work if she doesn't say it aloud.

Sometimes it doesn't work even when she does.

Without Corey, scary things can creep in no matter how snugly she tucks the bedding; no matter how tired she is when her head hits the pillow.

She'd learned long ago to cram every waking minute with work, books, exercise, errands, socializing . . . anything to keep busy. When you're idle, there's room in your brain for memories. That leaves her utterly exhausted most nights— including this one, three hours from her own time zone with city sounds and sirens, thunder and rain beyond the window.

Before crawling into her side, she seals the sheets and blankets on the opposite side all the way from the vacant pillow adjacent to her own to the foot of the bed where her dogs are curled up, already asleep.

"May the dreams you hold dearest be those that come true," she whispers into the dark, and closes her eyes.

But tonight, there are no dreams.

Tonight, only nightmares.

LEILA

Los Angeles

When her phone vibrates late Wednesday evening, Leila Randolph is curled up with the cats on the gray sectional, binge-watching *Real Housewives*.

Her first thought—*hope*—is that it's a text from Stef. But no, she'd broken off communication with him weeks ago.

It definitely isn't Gib, asleep upstairs, his snores occasionally audible over the television.

Maybe it's one of her daughters. Ellie and Kate are in Anaheim with their dad, courtesy of a joint custody arrangement between Leila and her ex.

More likely, it's yet another credit card company or bank reminding her that another payment is overdue.

Leila nudges the cats from her lap, finds her phone between the cushions, and sees not a text, but a reminder from herself: **Check numbers**. It's one of the many calendar alerts that pop up daily, courtesy of an electronically organized life with too many moving parts.

"Well, you know what *you* are?" one Botoxed brunette shrieks at another on TV.

Check numbers.

What does that even mean?

Stumped, Leila swaps the phone for her glass of cabernet and settles back to watch the tequila-fueled Housewives bicker over who gets to sit where on the private plane to the Caribbean and who gets which of several master suites in their rented seaside villa.

Must be nice. For her own girls' getaway last weekend, she'd scrimped for a back row middle airline seat and shared a no-frills Las Vegas hotel room with her friends J.J. and Molly, two fellow *real* housewives.

The Labor Day weekend trip marked exactly twenty-two years since they'd met as college freshmen at Northwestern University and established an instant bond upon discovering they all had birthdays the following week—Leila on the twelfth, J.J. on the sixteenth, Molly on the eighteenth.

They called themselves the September Girls, after the song—which was actually titled "September *Gurls*," but J.J., an English lit major, wasn't big on alternative spelling.

"We have to celebrate together every year, just like this, y'all, promise?" Molly had drawled the weekend before their eighteenth birthdays, as they took turns swigging from a bottle of bubbly swill.

"Maybe not *just* like this," Leila said. "We'll have real champagne. The good stuff. Or at least, better stuff."

"Yeah, and we won't need fake IDs to buy it," J.J. added.

"Okay, but same time next year! And every year. Promise?"

They promised.

They kept it throughout their college years. When they turned twenty-one, they bought three gold necklaces with small sapphire pendants, their shared birthstone— September Girls forever together in spirit no matter where life landed them.

After graduation, dispersed across the country, they'd settled on celebrating only milestone birthdays in person. They managed to reconnect for their twenty-fifth, missed their thirtieth, and decided thirty-five wasn't necessarily a milestone. Everyone was either broke, or busy with their own lives, or both.

We need to do something amazing when we hit the big 4-0, Molly had written last spring in their group text.

I'll start planning! Leila replied.

Vegas was her idea. The others had never been there and had some reservations.

"Guys, it's perfect for us," Leila had assured them in a group Zoom meeting. "The weather's nice, it's easy for us all to get to, there are plenty of hotel bargains, and there's a lot to do."

"Like slot machines?" J.J. asked.

"We don't have to gamble. There are shows, great restaurants, the hotel pool . . ."

"So we're going to Vegas and we're not going to any casinos? What's the point in that?" Molly asked.

"We can go to casinos. We'll each designate a certain

amount of money we can spend on gambling and when it's gone, it's gone. They give you free drinks while you're at the tables, and if you win enough, you get a lot more than that."

J.J. snorted. "Yeah, like a fraction of our money back."

"Or all of it. Or if you hit it really big, they might give you a dinner voucher or even comp the room."

"Has that ever happened to you?" Molly asked.

"Not yet," Leila said, as if she were an old Vegas pro. In truth, she'd only been there twice.

Once when she and Warren eloped, and again more recently on a stolen weekend with Stef. The first time, she and Warren lost the entire nest egg they'd saved up to buy furniture. The second time, she'd told Gib and the girls she had a training seminar for her joke of a job, and had been plagued by guilt before, during, after, and even now.

Not because she was cheating on Gib, because he isn't her husband and they're in an open relationship—his preference, not hers. Not even because she'd lied to him and the girls, because that was less messy, less complicated than the truth. It was for everyone's benefit.

No, she feels guilty on behalf of herself. Guilty because she deserves so much better, and having learned long ago that this world never bestows the things you deserve, she'd promised herself that she'd never settle. Yet she does, over and over.

So, Vegas. Again. Hoping the third time might be the charm.

"Wow. Free drinks, free dinner, and a comped room? I really hope one of us gets lucky," Molly said.

They hadn't, collectively losing every predesignated gambling dollar in the first casino on the first day. That didn't deter them from imagining how they could have spent a make-believe jackpot, and not just on luxuries. For all of them, a windfall would alleviate the burdens of debt, failed marriages, curtailed careers, and a pervasive feeling of powerlessness.

Leila had told them about losing her business, a high-end clothing boutique she'd envisioned as the next Fred Segal, and about the subsequent fruitless search for an adequate job and moving in with Gib because she had few other options. *No* other option.

J.J. shared that she and John had always dreamed of buying a house of their own with a home office where she could finally write her novel, and of sending their son to college and keeping him close by. Instead, they're stuck in the same urban apartment in a decaying neighborhood, with Brian enlisted and deployed in a distant land.

Theater major Molly had given up on Hollywood stardom years ago, but found a measure of contentment in marriage and success in regional theater, only to have the pandemic curtail her career and unplanned pregnancy do the same to her marriage.

Three lives riddled with bad choices early on that hadn't allowed them additional choices. Or perhaps, just riddled with bad luck.

Ah, now she remembers what *Check numbers* is about.

In the next commercial break, she looks around for

her carry-on from the trip and finds it right where she'd dropped it after a delayed flight home Monday night.

Maybe some part of her subconscious couldn't bear to empty the bag and return it to the closet shelf. Maybe, packed and waiting by the door, it's a reminder that it is possible to escape this life.

She'd been desperate to get away from her daughters after a flurry of back-to-school preparations. She loves them in the innate, visceral way that a mother loves her children, but in adolescence, they've grown difficult to *like*.

And yes, she also needed to get away from Gib. He may not be a churlish adolescent, but he's kicked off a new semester at the community college where he teaches philosophy and assumes that she's as fascinated by his revised syllabus as he is.

She even needed to get away from the cats, who claw the couch instead of their scratch post and throw up hairballs on the rug; away from rearranging pillows to hide the thread pulls, and cleaning barf stains morning, noon, night.

Away from endless household tasks and cooking meals for people whose dietary needs change without warning for no apparent reason—one daughter gone gluten-free one day, the other on a Paleo diet the next, Gib prone to juice cleanses, fasts, and occasional veganism.

Away from the claustrophobic condo she'd once found welcoming and the mundane job she'd been forced to take after her dream business failed and the dry heat and smoke that cloak Southern California at this time of year like an ugly wool sweater on a supermodel.

Away from endless days filled with far too many obligations and not nearly enough choices.

Away, away, away . . .

Leila rifles through the bag and finds a copy of *People* magazine she'd read on the plane home. Tucked between the pages is a makeshift bookmark: a lottery ticket for the unprecedented billion dollar Dealin' Dice jackpot.

She and her friends had chipped in to buy it on the way to the airport.

"It'll give us something fun to think about," Leila told them. "Maybe we'll win enough to cover a nice dinner for our next birthday trip."

"Or the trip itself," J.J. said. "We can go to the Caribbean. Hell, we can buy a Caribbean island, if we get the billion. What should we name it?"

"September Girls' Island, of course," Leila said.

"That doesn't sound like a real island."

"Sure it does. Like Gilligan's Island."

"*That's* a real island?" J.J. asked.

"September is hurricane season, y'all," Molly pointed out. "Maybe that's not the best name for a tropical island."

"Well, we'll make sure it's not in the hurricane zone. And it should have a volcano, like Gilligan's. But no quicksand."

"Definitely no quicksand," J.J. agreed. "I feel like I've been stuck in quicksand my whole life."

"Same here. What do y'all think the odds are of winning the jackpot?"

"Probably better for Lucky Leila than other people."

"You know I hate that nickname, J.J."

"I thought you just hated your brothers for giving it to you."

"If I were truly lucky, I'd have been born a man. Or at least, born into a family that wanted me."

"You *were* wanted," Molly reminded her just as she had in the old days, whenever Leila felt sorry for herself.

"Not by my brothers. Or my birth parents."

J.J. patted her hand. "You don't know that. Maybe they were forced to give you up."

"If they were forced, why would they insist on a closed adoption? Wouldn't they want to know where I am and that I'm okay? Or maybe have a chance to meet me someday?"

Back then, that would have been Molly's cue to tell Leila to look at the bright side, pointing out how blessed she was to have been adopted by a pair of wealthy Chicago surgeons, who after having three biological sons believed a daughter would complete their family.

That was before her adoptive parents cut her off from their money and out of their lives because she'd chosen to pursue her own dream instead of the goals they'd laid out for her.

Now bright-side Molly said instead, "If we win the lottery, you can hire a detective and find your roots. Come on, it's only a dollar each."

It was a dollar more than they'd budgeted for gambling, but they bought the ticket anyway.

As Leila tosses the magazine into the recycling bin,

another paper rectangle flutters from the pages. It looks almost like another ticket, but no, they'd only bought one. This is a photo strip from one of those old-fashioned booths.

We need an official September Girls portrait, y'all! Molly had shouted when they spied it in Vegas after a late dinner and too many drinks.

Leila returns to the couch with the photo strip and the lottery ticket, and searches for the Dealin' Dice website on her phone. It takes forever to load, thanks to millions—billions?—of fellow would-be billionaires attempting to check the numbers in this moment. Meanwhile, the House-wives are back from commercial break and bickering as they set sail on a luxurious yacht to a tropical paradise that isn't called September Girls' Island.

Leila forgets all about Dealin' Dice until the show goes to the next commercial. Now six bedazzled numbers are displayed on the lottery's home page, and the first two are familiar.

09, the number she and her friends had chosen for their mutual birth month.

12, Leila's own birthdate.

She looks down at the ticket. Yep: *09, 12 . . .*

Well, that's good. Maybe they've recouped their three-dollar investment.

The next two numbers printed on the ticket are 16 and 18, J.J. and Molly's September birthdates.

She checks her phone and her eyes widen.

Those two, as well, are listed on the Dealin' Dice site banner!

A quadruple match? How much is that worth? Probably enough for a nice birthday dinner next year; maybe more.

The last two numbers they'd chosen were 40, their current age, and 46, the number on their college dormitory door.

She holds her breath as she looks from the ticket to the screen.

There they are. Both of them.

She double-checks. Triple-checks.

09-12-16-18-40-46 on the screen.

09-12-16-18-40-46 on the ticket.

J.J.

Saint Louis

J.J.'s eyes fly open when her cell's jaunty ringtone yanks her from a hushed refuge.

The room is dark but for the faint glow of the digital alarm clock on John's side of the bed: 11:57 p.m.

"Babe?"

Beyond the window screen, distant sirens wail in the night. This is Saint Louis. There are always sirens.

"The phone is— Babe?"

She sits up and pats the adjacent pillow. John isn't in bed beside her. Where is he? Isn't it a weekend? If it's a weekend, he must be here. Weekends, he's off.

Her brain fog lifts, and she remembers.

It isn't the weekend. She'd been away for that—Labor Day, in Vegas, with Leila and Molly. She'd gotten home on Monday night, so this is Tuesday, or . . .

Wait, no. This is Wednesday, cresting Thursday.

The phone is ringing, ringing . . .

These days, everyone she knows communicates by text message. Only robots call, and strangers. Most are spammers, though some—well, *one*—had urgent news, on a cold December night.

It will never be over. It lies in the past. There's a huge difference.

Leila's words, just last weekend when they were discussing her adoption trauma.

And yes, things have been better for J.J. The long, bleak winter had overstayed as always, giving way to a wet, chilly spring too closely followed by a relentlessly muggy summer. September brought a long-standing plan come to fruition.

The Vegas getaway had been a welcome reprieve for J.J., blistering sunburn and all. She'd spent the weekend reconnecting, reminiscing . . . and forgetting.

For a little while, she was able to pretend everything was okay; able to convince herself, and her friends, that her life is . . . well, certainly not *phenomenal*, Molly's current adjective du jour.

Molly and Leila know, better than anyone, that her life has never been phenomenal.

I'd settle for normal. Normal would be good.

"Tell me everything!" Leila had said the first day, as she does. Back in college, after one of them had come back from a party or a date or a final, Leila would be there, waiting, expecting to be told—well, everything, even if you weren't the kind of person who was comfortable sharing much of anything.

But Leila was famous for asking questions and not

waiting for the answers, or answering them herself, and anyway, "Tell me everything" isn't a question.

And J.J. wasn't about to say "Everything is hard. It's all falling apart. I'm falling apart."

Anyway, that's not the truth. Somehow, she's managed to hold everything together.

But now her phone is ringing, and midnight calls never bring good news, and those damned sirens are wailing closer.

She grabs the phone and looks at caller ID, then answers, bracing herself.

"Hello? Leila? What—"

Incoherent screaming erupts on the other end of the line.

MOLLY

Savannah

Molly doesn't drink bourbon.

These days, she rarely drinks at all, having given up her nightly pinot grigio while she was pregnant. Her son is ten months old and weaned, but she still has seven pounds of baby weight to lose and should be avoiding empty calories.

Can't get emptier than this, she thinks, pouring two fingers of honey-colored liquid into a tumbler. Her trembling hand sloshes some onto the polished cherry and cypress desk, a prized family heirloom repurposed as a liquor cabinet. She ignores the spill, along with Ross's warning to wipe it up before it destroys the finish.

He lives in Buckhead full-time now, so his voice is only in her head, an earworm that lingers long after the song is silenced. A former favorite song that now grates.

She swallows the bourbon in a throat-scorching gulp and plunks down the empty glass like a saloon cowboy ready for another round.

She shouldn't. Dawson will be up at dawn, teething, fussy, demanding every ounce of her energy. Yet she pours again, and oops, spills again.

Dammit, Molly! Earworm Ross scolds. *That's a priceless antebellum antique!*

Yeah, well, it had survived the war; it'll survive a splash or two of Maker's Mark.

Their marriage hadn't survived her pregnancy. Sometimes she wishes that it had, on nights when she lies awake in the too-large, too-quiet house, missing . . .

Not Ross. She doesn't miss *him.*

No, she misses the stability of marriage—financial, and otherwise. Mostly financial, because it's not as if Ross would be helping her with the baby. His presence would make her life more exhausting and difficult in so many ways.

Her parents reminded her of that just days ago when they came to stay with the baby while Molly was in Vegas.

"You're better off without him," Mom said firmly.

"Better off raising a son alone, without a father?"

"You've got me for that, sugar," Daddy told her. "And remember, you're not alone. We're here, whenever you need us."

It's true, but how much longer can she rely on her parents? They help with everything from babysitting and household repairs, and they've offered to take her and Dawson into their one-bedroom Pooler condo in two weeks when she's forced to vacate this place.

She has yet to find an affordable alternative here in Savannah, but the last thing she wants is to complicate and crowd her parents' lives. They're getting up there in years and raised five daughters, Molly the youngest. They've been through enough.

At sixty, her father was diagnosed with a rare cancer. His only hope was to try experimental treatments his health insurance refused to cover, as the odds against survival were astronomical. His wife and daughters wouldn't hear of any other decision, and it ultimately saved his life. But the expense and subsequent global recession decimated his investments and savings, and residual health issues forced him into early retirement, reminding them all that life is precarious.

Things change. People you love and need aren't going to be around forever. They age. Leave. *Die*.

Again, Molly lifts the glass to her mouth, hand still shaking; her whole body shaking as it has been ever since Leila called.

There are no guarantees. In an instant, everything you ever knew about your life, every plan you ever made and every vision you ever had for your future, disappears. You pee on a stick—or answer the phone—and *poof!* Just like that, it's gone. All of it.

The bourbon slides down her throat and attempts to push her legs right out from under her. She sinks into a chair.

Goodbye, Abandoned Wife/Teetotalling New Mom Molly. Hello . . .

Whoever, whatever, she's going to be from now on.

Hello, and welcome back to *Disappearing Acts*. I'm host Riley Robertson, former investigative reporter, current podcaster, and perennial snoop!

This week, we're continuing our investigation into Hollywood's most intriguing mystery: *Whatever Happened to Chantal Charbonneau?*

For today's episode, we're going to take a closer look at the fascinating woman behind the myth and find out who she really was. At least, we're going to try. Sometimes, when you ask a question, you wind up with more questions than answers.

That's the case with Chantal Charbonneau.

For starters, that was a stage name. No one knows the real one, or exactly where she'd come from. Her past was shrouded in mystery. The only details we have are the precious few she chose to reveal.

Her official bio stated that she'd been born in 1961 in France, was orphaned at a young age, and was shipped off to her only living relative, an elderly cousin in Louisiana's bayou country. She was in her teens when the cousin died. Finding herself alone in the world once again, she took a bus to Los Angeles. She started using the name Chantal Charbonneau, found work waiting tables, and took acting lessons.

Chantal never shared specifics about where she'd lived in France or Louisiana, claiming she didn't like to talk about her childhood because it was so painful.

Yet her natural speaking voice bore no trace of a French or Cajun accent.

And though the tabloid press did its share of scouring for people from her past—and I'm sure some were willing to pay for information—as far as we know, no one ever came forward to reveal her true identity.

Some of you might think this is remarkable. How could one of the most famous, most photographed celebrities in the world go unrecognized by those who knew her when?

By the same token, how could one of the most famous, most photographed celebrities in the world go missing?

The only way that could happen, most people believe, is that she's dead.

But what if she's not?

Before you dismiss the idea, remember this: Chantal was an extraordinarily gifted character actress and, as such, an expert in disguise. She wholly transformed herself into the women she portrayed—not just gaining or losing weight, dyeing or cutting her hair, learning a new dialect, but literally seeming to become someone else, someone who bore no resemblance to herself. She received two Oscar nominations: one for playing an Austrian Holocaust victim, the other for a comedic turn as a wisecracking Brooklyn makeup artist.

That's why no one from her past ever recognized her and came forward.

She was a true chameleon, my friends.

And chameleons regularly shed their skin.

THURSDAY

LEILA

Still clutching the winning ticket, Leila paces from one end of the kitchen to the other. It's a galley design, so the distance is short, made shorter by the cats sprawled at one end and Gib at the other, barefoot and in boxer shorts, making coffee.

He'd been asleep when her shrieks roused him. So, apparently, had the next-door neighbor, Mrs. Martinez, who'd responded with the usual thumps on the shared wall with what sounds like a battering ram.

He peers into a can of Maxwell House. "Almost empty."

"There's another one."

Checking the cabinet, he says, "There are *three*."

"I had a coupon—buy two, get one free. So I stocked up."

"Well, now that you've won a billion dollars, your coupon days are over."

"A *third* of a billion dollars, and shouldn't you be making decaf instead?"

He turns to give her an incredulous look.

A bearded, bespectacled philosophy adjunct, he's pedantic in a way she finds charmingly quirky, especially when compared to her slapdash ex. They may not have smoldering passion, and Gib made it clear from the start that he doesn't believe in marriage, or even monogamy. But for now, he's what she needs—a landing spot in a life turned Tilt-a-Whirl.

She gestures at the coffee can. "Gib, you *know* I have insomnia. You *know* I can't even have caffeine after ten in the morning without being awake all—"

"Seriously? Do you actually think you're going to *sleep* tonight?"

Reality dawns. Of course she's not going to sleep tonight. The way her heart has been racing since she saw those six numbers, she might never sleep again.

Then again, this might be the end of her chronic insomnia. Every problem that keeps her up at night stems from the financial instability that's plagued her in the two decades since her parents cut her off.

They'd expected her to come crawling back home after a taste of life without their funding. Her mother called daily and even her father reached out to her a time or two, offering what Molly called an olive branch and Leila considered a bribe. Her older brothers, all of whom had dutifully followed their predesignated academic and professional paths, took turns trying to strong-arm her into acquiescence, basically accusing her of being an ungrateful spoiled brat—nothing new.

Whatever Lucky Leila wants, Lucky Leila gets.

Lucky Leila has Mom and Dad wrapped around her little finger.

Lucky Leila thinks she rules the world.

She'd heard it all, all her life, and she needed a break.

She hadn't regretted her decision to go forward on her own terms, even a few years into the estrangement when she stumbled across her own name in an online search, listed as a survivor in her mother's obituary. The death had been sudden, months earlier. Maybe her father and brothers had been too shattered to track her down and let her know. Maybe they just hadn't bothered.

Leila had made her choice. She accepted the repercussions and resisted what-ifs.

Until recently, anyway.

If she'd reconciled with her family—if she wasn't the kind of person who just lets go—she might have worked harder to save her failing marriage.

If she wasn't still saddled with student loan debt she'd racked up after her parents stopped paying her tuition, she might have kept her clothing boutique afloat when the pandemic shuttered it. Or, she could have waited for subsequent employment worthy of her education and experience instead of accepting the one measly offer that came her way, a commission-based entry-level sales position.

Then she wouldn't be so infuriated by her ex-husband's new job, a position he'd landed with minimal effort and for which he's underqualified and overpaid, and his second wife and new family get to reap the benefits.

If Leila were being paid what she's worth, she and the girls would have found a home of their own when the landlord raised the rent, instead of moving in with Gib so early in their relationship.

If they weren't all crowded into a two-bedroom one-bath condo, constantly on each other's nerves, their relationships would be healthier: Leila's with Gib, Gib's with the girls, the girls' with each other and especially with Leila.

More than anything, she resents the growing tension with her daughters. She'd intended to be the opposite of her own mother—either of her mothers, including the biological one she'd never known. *She* would always be there for her children and love them unconditionally; a warm, tolerant, patient mother who would appreciate them for who they are and who in turn would be adored and respected.

Things may have started out that way, but these days, when the girls aren't picking arguments with her, criticizing her, and ignoring her rules, they're eyeing her with disdain she finds even more painful than outright opposition. Even sweet-natured Kate, who'd sworn just months ago never to sneak around or lie or treat Leila the way Ellie does, has become problematic.

You used to be nice, she grumbled recently.

Yeah, well, so did you, Leila shot back.

Kate was right, though. She really had been nicer, back when the girls were younger and Leila and Warren were amicably separated and her dream business was a goal within reach. There never seemed to be enough money even then, but at least she'd lived paycheck to paycheck instead of on credit and loans.

Everything has been so damned difficult for so long. So unfair.

This windfall won't right all the wrongs in Leila's past any more than it will cure the girls' adolescent angst, but it will help. Money can provide necessities, conveniences, and luxuries. Those things in turn can buy time, space, patience, freedom, peace of mind, sleep. . . .

She looks down at the precious, precious ticket, then strides toward her desk in a corner of the living area.

"What are you doing?" Gib asks.

"Putting this in a safe spot." She opens the only drawer fitted with a lock, which she never uses. She tucks the ticket into her checkbook and finds the key, buried in another drawer amid office supplies and fast-food condiment packets.

After double-checking to make sure the ticket hasn't somehow vanished from her checkbook, she locks that drawer and then glances around for a place to hide the key, conscious of Gib watching her.

"How about there?" he asks, pointing at the calendar hanging on the kitchen wall. "You can hang it behind the calendar."

"Good idea."

She hangs the key on the nail and replaces the calendar. It's filled with print ads for local businesses that had survived the pandemic, unlike her own, and the black Sharpie slashes Gib marks across every day that passes as if he's counting down toward some nonexistent event. He has no explanation for why he does it, other than that he always has.

That's Gib. And it shouldn't bother her—that little quirk—but it does. Even now. Especially now.

He pulls the recycling bin from under the sink to deposit the empty coffee can, and something catches her eye. "Wait!"

Before he can shove the bin back under the sink, she leaps from the stool and grabs the copy of *People* magazine she'd tossed in earlier.

She finds an article and shows it to Gib. "Look! I can't believe the coincidence."

"What coincidence?"

"If I hadn't read this the other day, I wouldn't have even known there was such a thing as a sudden wealth consultant. It's like fate put her on my radar so that I could hire her."

He leans in to look. "Chantal Charbonneau . . . Isn't she an actress? And—isn't she dead?"

"Missing. Declared dead, years ago."

"Maybe you should hire someone else," he says, deadpan.

"I am. I'm hiring *her*." She points at a photograph in the sidebar.

It shows a petite, olive-skinned woman with jet-black hair and cobalt eyes. The deliberate pose—arms folded, leaning against a stop sign.

Shea Daniels's advice for anyone dealing with an unexpected fortune: Stop!

The caption hadn't resonated with Leila when she'd first glanced at the photo on the plane. Now it does.

"Who is she?" Gib asks.

"Shea Daniels. She owns the estate where Chantal was living when she vanished, and she runs a sudden-wealth consultancy."

"Which means . . ."

"Which means she helps people deal with coming into a vast amount of money."

"Deal with it? You mean spend it."

"Spend it, invest it, save it, donate it. People who are born rich know how to manage it, but regular people need professional help."

"So this woman, Shea—she's, what? An investment specialist? A lawyer?"

"A consultant," Leila repeats, skimming the sidebar about Shea's business. "She runs a full-service agency that works with people who unexpectedly come into a fortune."

"Lottery winners."

"Not just lottery winners. All kinds of people."

"People who . . . what? Unearth a chest of gold doubloons?"

"Or stumble across a priceless masterpiece at a garage sale. Or they get a huge inheritance from a long-lost relative, or win a massive insurance settlement or lawsuit, or become an overnight media sensation like Cyphyr."

"Like what?"

"Cyphyr. She's a *who*, see? One of Shea Daniels's clients." Leila points to a photo of a scantily clad young woman pouting at the camera.

This may be the first Gib's heard of her, but she's on the

magazine's cover, and Leila's girls are avid followers, with the reverence Leila's generation had reserved for boy bands.

"No first name, or no last?" she'd asked her daughters the first time they brought her up. "Just . . . Cyphyr? As in . . . Cher?"

"*Share?*" Ellie echoed, as if Leila had lapsed into a foreign tongue. "What do you mean?"

Leila sighed. "Forget it. So it's Cyphyr as in . . . what? As in she's a *cypher?*"

"Yes, but she spells it with a *y*," Kate said.

"Well, that's how it's spelled. C-y-p—"

"She spells it with two *y*'s," Ellie cut in. "No *e*."

"Yeah, because she's not into vowels," her sister said solemnly.

"She's not into . . ." Leila shook her head, thinking of J.J., who'd vetoed September *Gurls* so long ago. "And why is this Cyphyr so famous?"

"Um, because she's an *influencer?*"

"But what does she actually *do?*"

Kate sighed and looked at Ellie.

Ellie sighed and said, "She doesn't *do* anything. She just, you know . . ."

"Influences?"

"Mom! That's random. She just . . ." Kate paused, searching for the right word.

According to Ellie, that word was ". . . *is*."

"She just *is?*" Leila echoed. "And *I'm* random? Trust me, ladies, people who just *are* won't get very far in life. Especially female people. We have to *do*."

The caption under her photo in *People* proves her wrong, citing Cyphyr's three-year eight-figure contract to join the cast of a popular NBC drama.

Asked whether she'd always wanted to be an actress, the young woman told the reporter, "I don't even want to act now. But they want me, and their ratings are going to be sky-high, so why not?"

Gib bends closer to the magazine, peering at the photo and the caption, and shakes his head.

"What?" Leila asks.

"You know how I feel about celebrity culture. Why don't you find a reputable financial planner instead of hiring someone you read about in a gossip magazine?"

She tells herself that he doesn't mean it in a condescending way; that he considers her an intellectual equal; that she *is* that and more, dammit. She's an intelligent, well-educated, resourceful woman whose parents had disowned her, whose husband had divorced her, whose business had failed, yet she's persevered, building a career, raising two strong young women, keeping a roof over their heads and food on the table.

"This isn't about hiring a financial planner, Gib."

"But you said—"

"Shea Daniels does a lot more than that. Here, listen to what she says."

She turns a page in the magazine and reads aloud, "'For an ordinary person coming into extraordinary financial gain, the key word is caution. Don't tell anyone about it, don't quit your job, don't spend on big purchases . . . basically, fight every natural impulse you have. You aren't yet equipped to handle a fortune. That's where I come in. My agency, Windfall, will help you avoid missteps that could cost you dearly—not just money or relationships, but your life.'"

"Your *life?*" Gib echoes. "Leila—"

"This is complicated, Gib. I need her, and I'm going to hire her."

"Don't you think you should consult J.J. and Molly first?"

"They'll be fine with it. I've always been the detail person. I planned our entire trip last weekend."

"What does that have to do with winning a billion dollars?"

"Gib, I'm perfectly capable of—"

"You're the most capable person I've ever known. But this isn't about planning a vacation, okay? You have no experience in this."

"Neither do you."

"I'm just trying to point out that you probably shouldn't make presumptions about people you haven't even seen in, what? Twenty years?"

"I saw them a few days ago, and they're my best friends, not just . . . *people.* I don't know why you're trying to start trouble."

"I'm not. I just want to make sure you don't . . ."

"What?" she asks when he trails off.

"You know you can be a little . . . never mind."

"A little what?"

"You might want to . . . dial it back a bit. That's all I'm saying."

"I can be a little *what?*"

His expression is benign, but she sees the shift in his jaw as he shakes his head.

"I can be a little what, Gib?"

"A little controlling."

There it is. The word the girls choose whenever they don't like one of her rules.

Men do it, too. *Especially* men, all her life. Growing up, it was the word her older brothers used to describe her. The one Warren hurtled at her, about her, when their marriage began to disintegrate. Even Stef . . .

"You're a control freak, Leila, you know that?" he'd said back in April, before she broke up with him.

"What I know is that this world is pure chaos," she'd shot back. "And I know that you'd be a fool not to control the few things you can. Especially if you're a woman. Especially if you're me."

She doesn't bother defending herself to Gib because things are different now. Different than they were last spring, or yesterday, or even an hour ago.

Few things that mattered then will ever matter again. The pervasive powerlessness and frustration are gone.

For the first time in her life, she really is in control. She has choices.

Choices, at last.

SHEA

Shea is running through a deserted urban landscape, chased by grasping talons, when a familiar ringtone wrenches her free.

Opening her eyes to a digital clock glowing in the dark, she sees that it's much too late—or too early—for ringing phones. *And* barking dogs.

Well, one barking dog. At the foot of the bed, teacup Chihuahua Lola springs into a yappy commotion, while Irish wolfhound Mel doesn't stir.

"Lola! Shush! *Cállate!*"

With a final woof to show who's boss, Lola curls up beside Mel and closes her eyes.

Shea's frequent East Coast business trips have improved dramatically over the past year, now that she can travel with her dogs. She'd traded commercial flights for private jets and hotel living for this West 74th Street brownstone with a full-time caretaker on the ground floor, a large office on the first, and spacious living quarters above.

Still, after ten mostly rainy, humid days in the city with

an insufferable client, she's anxious to get back. Not to her Redondo Beach duplex where she keeps her surfboard or the Holmby Hills pied-à-terre near her West Coast office, though both residences, like this brownstone, are comfortably luxurious.

No, Shea longs for the stately villa perched on a precipice along the Central Coast. It's remote, and lacks a few modern amenities others might consider necessities. It's also steeped in mystery, quite possibly haunted, and purportedly cursed.

Yet for her, Windfall is a refuge, and it's home.

She'll be there in time for the weekend, barring disaster—though one might be brewing if her assistant is calling at this hour.

She grabs the phone and grumbles, "Seriously, Justin? It's five in the morning."

"It's only two here, and this is important."

"That's what you said the last time you called me."

"Hey, you can blame your pal Cyphyr for *that* interruption."

Cyphyr—whose real name escapes Shea and doesn't matter to the rest of the world—isn't a pal, but a recent client. At fourteen, she's become an overnight sensation, thrusting everyone in her orbit—including Shea—into the spotlight.

The piece in *People* was meant to publicize Windfall and attract new clients. *Legitimate* clients as opposed to little old ladies who want to know how much a vintage copper washtub might be worth, or Cyphyrmaniacs, as the teenage influencer's young fans refer to themselves.

For the most part, Justin can handle the current barrage of inquiries and issues, but this is the second time he's woken Shea in a matter of hours. Around midnight, he'd called to say, "I don't want to worry you, but Cyphyr is missing from her suite at the Ritz."

"Missing?"

"She ordered room service and when they delivered it, she didn't answer the door. Our security detail has been posted in the corridor all night and didn't see her leave, but now she's not answering calls or texts."

"Maybe she snuck out to go to a club or something."

"She hasn't. This is serious."

"How do you know?"

"Because her social media has gone dark. She hasn't posted a selfie in over an hour," Justin said gravely, as if reporting that someone had spotted Cyphyr bound and gagged in a car trunk.

As it turned out, she was safe and sound in her hotel suite, having fallen asleep while plugged into headphones blasting music, like any other overtired teenager.

"This had better not be another false alarm, Justin," Shea says now, around a deep yawn.

"It's not. I've got big news."

"You finally got a restraining order on that podcaster who keeps approaching you in the parking garage like Deep Throat?"

"Riley? I told you, she just wants to interview you for her book, and—"

"And I told *you* to let her know when *that's* going to happen, so if the big news is that hell has frozen over—"

"It hasn't. Listen, Shea, Dealin' Dice has a winning ticket."

"Whoa. That *is* big."

The jackpot has gone unclaimed for a few months now, creating a publicity frenzy as it grew to a historic ten-figure sum.

"Yeah. And the winner just called to hire you. She said she read about you in *People*."

She groans. "Justin, this is probably another ridiculous Cyphyrmaniac stunt. Some fan trying to—"

"No, Shea, I had her text me a picture of the ticket. It's legit. She just won a billion dollars."

"And she wants to hire me?"

"Yes. Well, *they* do. She bought the ticket with a couple of friends."

"Uh-oh. Group jackpots are always so complicated."

"I know, but she said they're like sisters."

"That's what they all say. Did you tell her—" She breaks off, hearing a loud crackling on the line. "What was that?"

He sighs. "Something's going on with the phones. Probably the fires."

"Are there any nearby?"

"Near enough. The Santa Anas are kicking in, and you know what that means."

Meteorologically speaking, the hot, dry winds exacerbate fire season. But many Angelinos claim that the so-called "devil winds" wreak other kinds of havoc, creating psychological anxiety and triggering violent crime spikes.

"I know what it means," she tells Justin. "Anyway, did you counsel our winner that she and her friends need to keep this a secret?"

"She already knew. She'd read the FAQ section on the website before she called."

"Then she's aware they'll need to—"

"Set up a trust before they claim the money. She knows."

"And you pointed out—"

"That the ticket is bearer-specific, so she'd better guard it with her life? Done."

Shea smiles. "Sounds like you've got everything under control. I'm flying home tomorrow, so let the team know, and arrange to get the lucky ladies to LA as soon as possible. They're sisters, you said?"

"No, they were college roommates. They hadn't seen each other in years until a reunion last weekend, which is when they bought the ticket. This woman—Leila—she's a talker. Kept going on about how they all get along perfectly and there won't be any problems, and how much they all love each other—lived together for four years, the money won't change anything between them . . . yada, yada."

Shea's gaze flicks to a framed photo on the dresser. Cast in a murky Kodachrome fade, a couple pose arm in arm in front of an Echo Park bungalow long before Echo Park or bungalows were trendy. Scrolled iron railing, vinyl siding, metal awning.

In poverty, they appeared not to have had a care in the world.

She turns away from the photo.

Leila is wrong about the money not changing anything between her and her friends. She'll find out soon enough that it changes everything—period.

J.J.

At a few minutes after eleven, J.J. stubs out her cigarette and sits down at her kitchen table to log into the Zoom meeting Leila had set up.

With a click of the mouse, she finds herself projected on-screen, looking like someone's kid sister. Her face is still blotchy from too much Nevada sun last weekend. Her brown hair falls to her shoulders, unbrushed since yesterday, and she's wearing the faded Cardinals T-shirt she'd slept in before the call that had subsequently kept her up all night.

While J.J.'s glasses seem to magnify her dark circles, Molly's blue eyes are shadowed and lined in cosmetics. She's so very *Molly*, looking as though she's fresh from hair, makeup, and wardrobe on a film set. Her pretty face is framed by honey blond waves and she's wearing a pink floral top that appears freshly pressed. Her son is beside her in a bouncy seat beneath a trapeze-like contraption strung with plastic toys. The backdrop is brocade wallpaper, lace curtains, and sun-dappled Spanish moss beyond, a drastic difference from the dim, cluttered kitchen behind J.J.

In the center square, Leila is dressed in a crisp white blouse and navy blazer, her long black hair in a neat chignon. She's wearing gold hoop earrings and the gold sapphire necklace she'd worn all last weekend, so disappointed when Molly and J.J. didn't think to wear theirs, or even bring them to the reunion.

She breaks off in the middle of whatever she was saying to address J.J. "There you are! I was starting to wonder if I'd given you the wrong info for your time zone."

J.J. briefly considers going along with that. But Leila is the type to double back and check on that, and she isn't the type to make careless mistakes.

"No, it was right," J.J. tells her. "Sorry I'm late. I was just busy."

"Don't tell me you went into the office?"

Now would be a good time to tell the truth—at least, part of the truth. Her therapist, Dr. Michaels, thought it would be a good idea. In J.J.'s last session before the trip, they'd even practiced how she would broach the subject with Leila and Molly.

She was going to say, *I haven't been completely honest with you. There are some things you should know . . .*

But Leila had only asked, "How's everything?"

And Molly had asked, "How's work?" And then she'd barreled on, "I miss work so much. I miss anything that gets me out of the house. But then when I am out of the house, I miss Dawson so much."

When the conversation meandered back to a spot where J.J. thought she might be able to confess that she'd lost her job, she opened her mouth and a lie tumbled out.

And so the trend continues.

"I . . . called in sick," she says now. "I'm late because I had to take another call."

"You didn't tell whoever it was what happened, did you?"

"It was John, Leila. He's my husband, so yes, he knows."

"I hope you made sure he won't let anyone else know what's going on . . ."

"Don't worry. He won't."

". . . because you have no idea how awful things can be if this gets out there before we're prepared. I read that—"

"Come on, Leila, do we really need to hear about awful things right now?"

Molly chimes in. "No awful things! We should be celebrating."

"And we will, as soon as the money is in the bank," Leila assures them. "I've been online all night figuring out how we should do it."

"Do what?" J.J. asks.

"Claim the money."

"How many ways are there?"

"You'd be surprised."

Leila goes on for a few minutes about trusts, partnerships, corporations, and limited liability companies. She's always chatty, but today she's especially wired, referring to a pad filled with scribbled notes.

Molly pulls her phone out of her pocket as if she's just gotten a text, or has simply lost interest.

If only they could have had this conversation in person like the old days, over happy hour margaritas or in their dorm, sprawled on a bed. Usually Leila's. J.J. never bothered to make hers, and Molly's was festooned in frills and heaped with too many stuffed animals and ruffled throw pillows.

In person, they'd be sipping champagne, giddy with excitement. Now they're together only on a laptop screen, captured in individual rectangles like the *Brady Bunch* sisters. Middle-aged Bradys steeped in shock and sleeplessness.

J.J. does her best to pay attention, wishing John were here. Not that he's ever been a financial wiz, by any stretch. But she's tired, and her head is spinning with unfamiliar details, and she needs a cigarette.

At last, Leila pauses to sip coffee. "So what do you think?"

Molly doesn't reply, texting on her phone.

J.J. says, "I think it all sounds really complicated."

"It *is* really complicated. That's the point. That's why we need to hire a sudden-wealth consultancy equipped to deal with UHNWIs—that stands for *ultrahigh net worth individuals*, in case you didn't know."

They didn't know. Or at least, J.J. didn't. Molly shakes her head, still texting.

"The good news is that I've already found someone, and you won't believe the coincidence." Leila holds a magazine up to the camera. "Remember Chantal Charbonneau?"

"Yes. What about her?" J.J. asks.

"Molly?" Leila sounds like a prickly teacher, and Molly looks up from her phone like a student who's been caught passing notes. "You're not even paying attention. You're busy . . . what are you doing? Texting someone?"

"Just my mom."

"You didn't tell—"

"No, I didn't tell her. You said not to tell anyone."

"Can the text wait a few minutes? We need to get this settled."

"Sorry. It was just her daily check-in and I didn't want her to worry." Molly puts her phone aside, then bends to wipe drool from the baby's chin with the edge of his bib.

J.J. is struck with a fierce pang of longing—for her son, for her mother.

Her own dawning days of motherhood, now blurred by time and distance, had been hazy even as she lived them. She'd lost her own mom just as she became one.

She should have been prepared. Her mother had been sick for a while. But the end came suddenly a few weeks before J.J.'s due date, as if her mom were vacating the spare bedroom to be used as a nursery for the grandson she never got to meet.

Now Brian is all grown up and deployed overseas, having enlisted in the Marines last year after high school graduation.

J.J. wants to tell Molly to bask in every precious moment of being a daughter to her mother and of parenting her child. But Leila is talking. Leila, it seems, is always, always talking.

One of her best qualities, J.J. had thought back when they first met, having spent the first eighteen years of her life struggling to overcome her shyness.

With Leila, there were no awkward conversational silences. With Leila, J.J. often couldn't hear herself think—a very good thing indeed back then, and many times since. Even now. Even on this day when fate has bestowed an unfathomable gift. When you've lost someone beloved, every happy moment is laced with longing for the person who'd have shared your joy.

"There was an article in *People* last weekend—any chance you guys read it?"

"An article about Chantal Charbonneau?" Molly asks.

"Well, she's mentioned—I mean, this week is the anniversary of her disappearance—but it's more about Shea Daniels, who lives at Windfall, Chantal's old estate. Windfall is also the name of the business she runs there. It's a sudden-wealth consultancy. Which is what we need. Which is why we need to hire her right away. Okay?"

The last word is so clearly an afterthought that J.J. is tempted to blurt that it's *not* okay; that Leila is steamrolling them, that this should be a group decision and they need time to make a proper one.

Dawson is the first to respond, with a whimper.

Molly quickly bends toward him, saying, "Sure, Leila. If that's what people do in this situation, then that's what we should do."

"Great. J.J.? Are you in?"

"How much does it cost?"

"Not a penny until we get our winnings, and then Windfall gets a percentage of that. A tiny, tiny percentage," she adds quickly. "Believe me, it's a drop in the bucket. So if we're all good with this . . . ?"

J.J. hesitates. Is she really going to argue against hiring a professional who knows how to handle a billion dollars?

You sure as hell have no idea where to start.

Anyway, the sooner she gets the money, the better.

The call she'd mentioned to Leila—the one that made her late for this meeting and made her reach for her cigarettes—had been from the bank.

The manager had asked to speak to John. J.J. said he wasn't available.

"When would be a good time to call back?"

"It's hard to say," she lied. "But it's a joint account, so . . . is there a problem?"

He informed her that it's overdrawn, making it clear that he doesn't believe she—or perhaps women in general—grasps the concept of balancing a checkbook. Which she certainly does. Unfortunately, that skill doesn't come with the power to make funds magically appear when you need them.

Now the funds have appeared—or are about to, anyway. The first thing she'll do when she gets her millions is deposit a massive check into her account, leave it there long enough for the condescending banker to take note, and then withdraw the whole amount and switch to a new bank.

"J.J.?" Leila prods. "Are you okay with Windfall?"

"Sure. Whatever you think is best."

"It's not just about what *I* think is best. We're all in this together."

"I know. I just . . . I can't quite believe this is happening."

"I can't, either," Molly says. "Are you positive all the numbers match, Leila? And the ticket is for the right date?"

"Of course I'm positive! Do you think I'd make a mistake about something like that?"

"Leila never makes mistakes," J.J. points out, and Leila frowns.

"Are you being sarcastic?"

"No," J.J. says, though she isn't entirely sure. She's so very tired, and Leila is so very . . . Leila-ish.

"Okay, well . . . seeing is believing. I'll be right back."

Leila vacates her on-screen rectangle, leaving Molly to focus on her baby and J.J. to gaze longingly at the cigarette pack on the cluttered counter.

Her friends don't know she's smoking again. Well, still smoking. More regularly lately than ever before.

She's pretty sure they wouldn't approve, even though they'd all done it, back in their college days. Watching her mother die of lung cancer probably should have sworn J.J. off the habit forever, but it was the opposite. Cigarettes ease her anxiety and, along with prescription medication, they've gotten her through some hard times over the years.

But better days lie ahead. Money will alleviate her most pressing problems and provide resources to tackle others.

If only it would solve them all.

LEILA

Earlier this morning, as Gib shuffled for the door with his car keys and travel mug, yawning deeply, Leila had suggested he take the day off and go up to bed.

"I can't do that at the last minute, especially this early in the semester."

"Oh, come on. It's just a job."

"And I have no intention of leaving it, no matter how this thing shakes out."

She suspected he was talking about their relationship, but wasn't about to go there with him. "Shakes out? You mean the ticket? It's not a mistake, Gib. We won."

"*You* won, Leila. Not me."

Well, yes. By *we*, she'd been referring to herself along with J.J. and Molly, not herself and Gib. Having spent hours reading up on financial and legal advice for lottery winners, she's aware that she needs to make that crystal clear.

Things would be different if he were her husband, but even if he believed in monogamy—which he does not—

remarriage would have meant Leila had to give up alimony from her ex.

Now she no longer needs Warren and his measly monthly checks.

Yet nor does she need Gib's domestic partnership.

After he left for work, Leila had retrieved the key from behind the calendar, the ticket from the drawer, and the empty coffee can from the recycling bin. She'd stashed the lottery ticket in it and put it back in the cabinet with the others. It isn't that she doesn't trust Gib. It's just . . .

You can't be too careful when the stakes are this high.

She grabs the coffee can and returns to the couch, crying out as her bare foot lands on a hair ball in a pool of cat vomit.

"Leila, honey? Are you okay?" Molly calls from the laptop.

"I'm fine." She rubs her foot against the sectional, leaving a smear on the upholstery,

Whatever. She can now afford to hire someone to clean up after the cats.

Wait, no—she can just get a new couch. A new everything. A new house, far from this dreary Valley condo where windows reveal nothing but other people's windows, distant hills typically obscured by smog, or—today—smoke.

She addresses Molly and J.J. "Drumroll, please?"

J.J. obliges with a fingertip beat on her table as Leila opens the plastic lid and reaches into the coffee can.

It's empty.

Her heart slams her ribs.

Somehow, someone stole the ticket.

Gib—it had to be Gib, or . . .

Windfall! She'd given them her name and . . . no, not her address, had she?

Anyone could have found that information, though. Anyone could have—

Ah, someone *could* have, but nobody *had*. When she tilts the coffee can for a closer look, the precious ticket drops out into her lap.

"Tada!" She holds it up to the screen.

J.J. stops thumping. "Wow! It's really real!"

Molly leans closer and reads off the numbers: "*09-12-16-18-40-46*. Oh, my goodness!"

Grinning, Leila tucks the ticket back into the coffee can.

"Hey, Leila?" Molly says. "That's probably not the best place to keep something that valuable."

"Don't worry. I've got a safe-deposit box. I'm bringing it to the bank."

"Wow, I didn't think anyone had those anymore."

"Warren and I got it years ago, when we got married. He wanted it for his grandfather's stamp collection."

"But what if someone goes into the safe-deposit box after you leave?" J.J. asks.

"That's illegal."

"You think that would stop some banker from stealing a billion dollars?"

"J.J., that's completely irrational! Nobody at the bank, or anywhere else, even knows I have it!"

"I wish you had a wall safe in your house," Molly says,

and indicates an oil portrait on the wall behind her, of an unsmiling young woman in ruffles and a snood. "There's one right behind that painting of Ross's great-great-great-someone-or-other. It's where they hid the jewelry and silver during the Civil War."

"No great-great-greats or safes here, unfortunately. And this is fire season. I can see smoke from my window. The wind can shift and the next thing you know, you've lost everything. We can't lose this. It has to go to the bank."

"I just wish Warren didn't have access to it," Molly says. "I'd never trust Ross not to go snooping into a safe-deposit box if we had one."

"Ross is a lawyer, and there were major assets involved in your divorce, and it isn't even final yet," Leila points out. "Ours was years ago, and Warren sold the stamp collection when he lost his job. I doubt he even has a key anymore. I'm sure he forgot all about it. Anyway, it's just for a few days. Shea wants you two to fly out Friday so that we can meet with her team and—"

"Wait, *Friday?*" J.J. cuts in. "You mean . . . *tomorrow?*"

"Yes. We can't claim the money until we hammer out the details and draw up and sign the legal documents."

"But . . . couldn't we meet in a more central location?"

"The ticket is in California, J.J., and so is Windfall."

Molly shakes her head. "I can't make it this weekend. We've got a family barbecue on Saturday at my parents' house."

"Molly! A barbecue? You can't be serious."

"You can't be serious about traveling again! I'm still exhausted from last weekend. I haven't even unpacked yet, and I'd have to pack today, and the only chance I'd have is when Dawson goes down for his nap, and my mom always says that when the baby naps, I should nap, too, and this might be my only chance to get some rest, and—"

"Molly, take a breath!" Leila says. "This is the most exciting thing that's ever happened to you. You can't sleep through it, and you can't miss it for a barbecue."

"Well, I can't pay for a flight to California or a hotel," J.J. says. "I'm broke after last weekend and my credit cards are maxed out."

Molly nods. "So are mine."

"That makes three of us, but we don't have to pay out of pocket for any of this. Shea's team is making all the arrangements."

"I was just away from him for four days," Molly says, clutching the baby, who squirms in her grasp.

"Why don't you bring him along?" J.J. suggests.

"Flying across the country alone with a baby would probably be even harder than leaving him," Leila says quickly. "I'm sure your parents would take him again, Mol."

"But if I can't tell them about the ticket, what would I tell them about why I have to fly to California on short notice?"

"Just make up something."

"Leila! You're suggesting I blatantly lie to someone I love?"

"You have no choice. You can't tell them the truth. Statistically, family and friends pose the biggest threat when someone comes into a windfall, and we're not supposed to tell anyone other than our spouses."

"Well, in case y'all forgot, I don't have a spouse anymore."

Leila opens her mouth, but J.J. cuts her off. "Gib's not your spouse, Leila, yet you told him. Why can't Molly tell her parents? You can't possibly think they're a *threat?*"

"Look, I can't keep anyone from doing anything. I'm just sharing Windfall's guidelines. It's for our own safety, and for our loved ones' safety. There have been abductions and—"

"Fine!" Molly cuts in quickly. "But I can't lie to my parents, so I'll just have to bring Dawson. Do you have a portable crib at your house, Leila, so I don't have to lug one on the plane?"

"We're not staying *here*! I told you, Windfall is setting it all up."

"Well, do you know which hotel? I need to make sure there's a crib."

"Not a hotel. We're staying at Windfall. The house," she adds, seeing their blank expressions. "It's up the coast, right on the ocean."

"You mean *the* house? The one where Chantal Charbonneau went missing? I don't know if I like that idea."

"You of all people should be into it, Molly. You're the one who was obsessed with her back in college."

"Y'all were, too. The whole world was obsessed."

"But you were obsessed even before she disappeared.

She was your inspiration for getting into acting, remember? You wanted to be just like her."

Molly shudders. "Well, I don't want to go to that house and disappear, or be murdered and thrown into the ocean."

"She wasn't murdered," Leila says firmly.

"She might have been. There were all those rumors about her being stalked by a deranged fan."

"Or losing her mind and jumping to her death," J.J. adds.

"That didn't happen, either."

J.J. raises an eyebrow. "Leila, nobody knows what happened. How do you?"

"I don't know for sure, but I did listen to the last season of *Disappearing Acts.*"

"What?" they ask in unison.

"You guys! You must have heard of the podcast—it's the one about famous people who have vanished?"

"Podcast? I barely have time to watch TV or read a book," Molly says.

"Well, the beauty of podcasts is that you can listen while you're doing other things. Anyway, the host—her name is Riley Robertson—featured the Charbonneau case and she really explores all the angles. The most plausible theory is that she just ran away and took on a new identity."

"With the whole world looking for her? And no one ever recognized her? That seems like the least plausible theory," J.J. comments.

"Not if you keep in mind that she was an amazing actress trained in transforming herself into someone else.

Plus, it happened a few days after 9/11, so the news kind of got swallowed up in that for a while. You both need to download the podcast and listen on the plane. It's so interesting. And Riley Robertson has this huge book deal to write about the case. You know, maybe we can do some sniffing around while we're at Windfall."

"Y'all can be Nancy Drew on your own time," Molly says. "I'd really rather stay somewhere else."

"It's not up to us. Shea is flying us out there and bringing her team to the house."

"When you say team . . . I mean, what exactly do they do?" J.J. asks. "Are they finance people? Attorneys?"

"Both. Plus there are people who handle real estate, security, publicity, travel, therapists . . . you name it."

From J.J.: "*Publicity?*"

From Molly: "*Therapists?*"

"Things get complicated when you come into this kind of money. Do you know how many people in our shoes wind up bankrupt or batshit crazy or dead?"

"*Dead?* I can't afford to be dead. I have a baby."

"I don't think any of us can afford to be dead," J.J. points out.

"It happens. I can tell you the crime statistics . . ." Leila flips a notebook page, scanning her scribbles. "There are extortions, kidnappings, suicides, murders . . ."

"Leila! This is supposed to be a dream come true. You're making it sound like a nightmare," J.J. tells her.

"It *is* a dream come true. It's going to be great."

"Then can we please stop dwelling on the bad stuff and just, you know, celebrate?" J.J. asks.

"Yes! I need to see y'all and have some champagne and caviar and a big old group hug."

"You got it," Leila says with a grin, thinking that there's no one in the world with whom she'd rather share this miraculous good fortune.

Then again, she supposes, in a perfect one, she wouldn't have to share it at all.

Hi, guys, welcome to *Disappearing Acts*. I'm host Riley Robertson, former investigative reporter, current podcaster, and perennial snoop!

In this week's episode, we'll continue this season's deep dive into Hollywood's most intriguing mystery: *Whatever Happened to Chantal Charbonneau?*

Setting is a key part of any mystery, as anyone who's ever read an Agatha Christie novel knows. By the way, Agatha was featured back in season two of this podcast, devoted to ten famous writers who vanished. Bet you didn't know there were so many, did you? Be sure to give it a listen!

Getting back to Chantal, today we're going to explore Windfall, her estate, which is the last place she was ever seen . . . unless you count sightings since her disappearance, everywhere from Palm Springs to Paris. But I'm getting ahead of myself.

Today's guest is Andrew Chapman, a member of the Southern California chapter of the Society of Architectural Historians. Welcome, Andrew! What can you tell us about Windfall?

Thank you, Riley. The house was built in 1929 by Hollywood mogul Drake Malcolm II, as a weekend retreat for his family. Drake's wife was silent film star Verna Garner, and they had three little boys with their mother's platinum blond ringlets and their father's devil-may-care swagger. The family represented the Hollywood A-list of their era, well-documented and photographed in the press.

Drake spared no expense on his dream house, and what could go wrong? California real estate was booming like everything else in that era of prosperity. He was on top of the world as that final summer of the Roaring Twenties gave way to autumn and his dream house came to fruition.

Then, in October, the stock market crashed. Drake's bravado had spawned increasingly reckless stock investments on margin, leaving him in financial ruin. Construction on Windfall came to a screeching halt. The exterior structure was finished, but the interior work had barely begun, and the landscape was a barren swath of dirt and rocks.

For well over a decade, the abandoned seaside mansion sat like a luminous shell washed up on a wreckage-strewn beach. Drake's wife left him. His boys grew up and enlisted. The middle son was killed on a Normandy beach, and the youngest shot down in the South Pacific. By the time the eldest returned to Los Angeles with a pregnant war bride, his father had drunk himself into an early grave.

In the 1950s, Drake III hired architects, construction teams, and interior designers to complete the work on Windfall. Once again, disaster struck—this time, a natural one, in the form of a demolishing earthquake.

Eventually, he rebuilt the house. By then, his wife had gone home to England with their two children. Windfall remained shuttered and vacant until his death in 1995.

Rumors that the place was cursed kept many prospective buyers away, but Chantal Charbonneau bought the property in September 1997 and became the home's first and only full-time occupant.

We all know how her story ended. Exactly four years after she took ownership of the estate, she vanished without a trace—yet another victim of the Windfall Curse.

FRIDAY

SHEA

So much for the smooth trip home and California sunshine Shea's been craving after a week in rainy New York City.

The flight had been turbulent, with a rough landing thanks to gusting Santa Anas, and LA is hot and shrouded in smog and smoke. The dogs had been uncharacteristically anxious on the plane and are wary even now, in the passenger seat of her Porsche Boxster.

"Hey, it's all good, guys," Shea tells them. "We're going home."

At least Cyphyr is out of her hair for a while. Having overseen the girl's transition into life as a UHNWI, she'd left her in good hands with the team.

She tries Justin on his cell and gets no answer. That's odd.

She tries the house phone. He answers on the third ring, sounding breathless. "Shea! Welcome home."

"Thanks. Are you on a treadmill?"

"No, but I was upstairs when I heard the phone ring.

My poor old bones are getting too old for this. It might be time to retire."

"You can't. I need you."

"Then I need *you* to install an elevator in this house. Or at least another couple of landline extensions."

"That can be arranged, my friend. So the service is down? Is it the fires?"

"Must be. There was cell service until a little while ago, but not anymore. No internet, either, and I'm guessing this line won't be working for long. Can you hear the static?"

"I can. I'll be quick. Did the cleaning staff make up all the rooms?"

"Yes, they were in and out last night."

"How about the space for the baby? Is everything there?"

"Based on what I know about babies—which is absolutely nothing—I can only tell you that there's a lot of . . . *stuff*. And the stagers did a nice job converting the dressing room to a nursery in a matter of hours."

"Is the kitchen stocked? And did you talk to the caterers about tonight's dinner delivery?"

"Yes, and yes. Everything is arranged."

"Thank you, Justin. I know you're probably anxious to get back to LA, but can you stay until I get there?"

"Of course. There's just one little thing . . ."

Uh-oh.

". . . Abi had a death in the family."

Abi Mizrahi is her West Coast security consultant, assisting clients with keeping themselves and their families safe as they adjust to their new status.

"I'm so sorry to hear that. His mother?" She'd been battling cancer, but last Shea heard she was in remission.

"No, his sister."

"I didn't know he had a sister."

"She was much younger—a junior at USC. It was a hit and run. She and her friends were leaving a club and a car barreled onto the sidewalk out of nowhere."

Shea clenches the wheel. She knows what it is to lose a sibling so young, violently and tragically . . .

"Shea? Are you there?"

"Yes. I'm here. Just . . . this is horrible. Let's see if there's anything we can do to make this as bearable as possible for Abi and his family. And about a replacement for the weekend—"

"Found one. I'm way ahead of you. I . . ."

The line dissolves into static.

"Justin? Are you there?"

More static, and then, "I'm here."

"Okay, well, we can't just use anyone. It has to be someone who knows how to handle . . ."

She pauses at a burst of static, realizing he can't hear her.

After a moment, she hears him say something. Or at least she thinks she does, but it makes no sense.

"Justin? Are you there? Hello?"

"I'm here! And I said I've already found someone and it's Beck, so you can relax."

Justin wouldn't use *Beck* and *relax* in the same sentence if he knew the whole truth.

"I thought he was in South America."

"He's been back in LA for a few weeks, and he was available. Guess it's our lucky day."

Yeah, not Shea's. Not anymore.

Justin tells her that Leila Randolph is already at the house and the others should be there shortly. Beck, financial advisor Elizabeth Fuentes, and attorney Morgan Brody are slated to arrive this evening, with the rest of the team not needed until tomorrow.

She hears him talking, but the words don't register, and not because they're interspersed with static.

Her brain is clogged with memories of a man she hadn't expected to see again so soon—if ever again. As of December, he'd been in Colombia on an assignment he said would keep him away for months, perhaps longer. He hadn't provided details; she hadn't asked questions.

Justin warns her that the trip to Windfall took much longer than usual today, with detours around the wildfires.

That's fine with Shea. She's in no hurry now that she knows Beck will be there.

"By the way, did you finish the book on the plane?" An avid crime fiction fan, Justin is referring to a buzzy novel he recently read and passed along to her.

"Not yet, and no spoilers, please."

"Don't worry. You'll never guess the twist."

"I'm pretty sure I already have, just like the last two books you gave me."

"But *this* is a major blindside."

"I have yet to be blindsided."

By a book, anyway.

Real life is a different story. Time and again . . .

And now Beck. Dammit.

She hangs up, gazing through the windshield at the swath of crimson brake lights against the gray landscape like spatters of blood on concrete.

MOLLY

Molly should have left the baby with her parents for the weekend. She should have trusted them with the truth, or even told them a harmless lie about why she was going away, as Leila had suggested. Sure, she'd have missed him, but anything would be better than today's travel ordeal and her guilt over having subjected him to a cross-country flight.

She'd anticipated that he might become irritable on the plane, yet had naively assumed a crying baby would somehow be less stressful in first class.

Wrong. Coach passengers have lower expectations, resigned to six hours of misery. Every time Dawson whimpered, Molly endured daggers from the people sitting around her, other than one well-heeled grandma who was full of useless, outdated advice that fell just short of suggesting that Molly shoot the child with a tranquilizer dart.

At least he's sleeping now, strapped into his car seat beside her in the back of a chauffeured SUV, on a coastal road climbing along increasingly rugged terrain.

Earlier in the trip, she'd caught brief glimpses of the

blue-gray Pacific Ocean melding with a filmy western sky, but visibility is low now that they're detouring around a massive wildfire. She'd rolled up her window to shut out the acrid smoke gusting on a hot wind, worried that it isn't good for the baby's lungs, or her own, for that matter.

Venturing into the burning wilderness can't be safe, can it?

Of course it isn't safe! You know it isn't safe! What are you doing here? This is crazy!

Californians deal with it, though—a fact of life, like earthquakes. Only more predictable, like hurricane season back home. You just learn to live with it.

Only she's not evacuating the coast; she's barreling right into the storm.

The fire isn't all that's making her uneasy, thanks to Leila and her talk about crime statistics and lottery winners.

What if Windfall is a scam and this whole thing is a setup? What if the man at the wheel isn't a driver, but an abductor?

Come on, Molly. This is real life, not a movie.

Still, she clutches her phone like a lifeline, cut off from the world without a cell signal. It had grown sketchy before disappearing altogether as she was texting with Leila, who's already at the house. She'd sent Molly and J.J. a photo of champagne chilling in an ice bucket, with the message, **Where are you guys? Don't make me drink alone!**

On my way! Molly wrote back, and Leila's reply came quickly, as usual: a thumbs-up emoji and **Yay! See you soon!**

Nothing from J.J. Her flight was scheduled to arrive ahead of Molly's. Maybe she, too, is incommunicado out here in the middle of nowhere. Or maybe she's been abducted, and Leila, too, and Molly is next.

The car makes an abrupt left off the highway toward what looks like a wall of flowering shrubs and she flings a hand out to protect her son.

This is it. They've veered off the road, being ambushed or—

No. She spies a tall iron gate, all but hidden by cascading scarlet bougainvillea. The car brakes and rolls to a stop alongside an electronic keypad. As the driver rolls down his window and enters a code, Molly spies an iron nameplate on the stone gatepost. It reads *Windfall*, the letters engraved in a vintage font that makes her think of flappers and *The Great Gatsby*.

The gate glides open and the car moves through.

She checks her phone. Ah, one bar. She types **I'm here!** into the group text, hits Send, and rolls down her window to a blast of hot air. The heat here, borne on a hot desert wind from the east, is so different from steamy late summer back home. It makes her uneasy, though the smoky smell has faded and the sun pokes through the misty clouds, bathing statues, benches, arbors, and a fountain in a pale, golden glow.

As they travel through a dense citrus grove and gardens alive with pollinators, she inhales a blossom-scented sea breeze. Perhaps a few bumblebees and butterflies along with it, because her stomach is fluttering and her thoughts buzz with a strange foreboding.

They emerge into a clearing, and there it is, a towering and invincible Spanish villa sheathed in stucco and wrought-iron opulence.

Molly's gaze goes to the rectangular turret that crowns the red tile roof.

A human figure is silhouetted in the window like a shadowy sentry.

She blinks and it's gone.

It must have been her anxiety-fueled imagination, or . . . an apparition?

Perhaps. She's never seen a ghost, but she believes in them. Her historic Savannah neighborhood is rich with paranormal lore that envelops Ross's home where she now resides, and the theater where she performed until the pandemic shuttered it forever.

Good old-fashioned Southern hauntings are one thing. An isolated California mansion with a suicidal or possibly murdered movie star phantom is quite another, though it makes perfect sense to Molly that Chantal Charbonneau would haunt this place.

The car pulls to a stop in front of the house. Molly looks down at her phone in her hand.

The solitary signal bar has disappeared once more.

J.J.

Seated in the back of a black SUV as a stranger navigates hairpin curves high above the sea, J.J. reminds herself that anxiety is to be expected when she ventures outside her comfort zone. These days, that's pretty much restricted to her apartment.

Dr. Michaels thinks she's bordering on agoraphobic. Maybe. And she's definitely always been aerophobic, having suffered through the two other plane journeys in her life: round trip to Puerto Vallarta for her honeymoon, and to Vegas.

She'd been frightened the first time even though John was with her. He'd never flown before, either, so they were equally terrified. Being together—and sipping tequila—had made that trip more bearable.

In advance of last weekend's girls' getaway, Dr. Michaels had reminded her to rely on the meditation exercises they'd practiced. He'd also prescribed a mild sedative in addition to her usual antidepressant and antianxiety medication.

It hadn't helped any more than the breathing exercises.

She'd have asked him for something stronger this time, but she couldn't tell him about this unexpected trip.

After some online research, she took a double dose for today's flight and found that it was more effective. Especially combined with free first-class champagne.

The flight wasn't awful, though she didn't fall asleep— probably due to a fierce nicotine craving. It seems wrong that smoking is forbidden in airports and on planes, the most anxiety-inducing places imaginable. Then again, you really can't smoke anywhere these days, yet another reason to stay home.

She'd been looking forward to a postflight cigarette at LAX, but the driver was waiting for her at the baggage claim. Having never ridden in a chauffeured vehicle, she isn't sure of the rules, but it hadn't seemed right to light up as he escorted her to the car, and certainly not after she'd climbed into the luxurious leather seat with yes, more champagne.

The bubbly failed to relax her this time, perhaps because too much time had elapsed since she'd taken her medication. She popped another dose—just one, a booster of sorts. But it's not working.

Recognizable civilization—the freeway, traffic, houses, strip malls, chain restaurants—has fallen away. On this coastal road high above the sea, there are no familiar landmarks; no other cars and no people. There is only rock and dirt, high walls and iron gates, unfamiliar vegetation blowing in a hot wind.

And there are fires.

Despite Leila's warnings and the electronic signboards

along the highway, J.J. had been caught off guard when they were forced to detour past manned barricades blocking off closed highways, and she'd glimpsed distant hillsides burning.

There are fires, and there is smoke, seeping into the car, though the windows are closed.

The driver, sealed up front behind a plexiglass panel, eyes masked by sunglasses, doesn't seem to notice. He's unfazed, breathing normally, unaware that an invisible noxious cloud is snaking tendrils around J.J.'s chest, lungs, heart, clouding her brain and her vision.

She keeps her fisted hands tucked under her legs to keep from banging on the divider and demanding that they turn around, or that he let her out of the car.

Where would she go, on a remote road in the middle of nowhere? One side is bordered by a steep incline, the other, a steep drop-off and no guardrail.

What is she doing in California, surrounded by a flaming foreign landscape, depending on a stranger to safely navigate a hazy hairpin road?

She shouldn't have let Leila talk her into this trip. She should have stayed home, surrounded by familiarity. Home, where it's safe, though even there, she's not immune to anxiety, panic, this impending sense of doom. Even there . . .

The wind could shift and the next thing you know, you've lost everything.

Here, the wind is incessant, thick with the same smoky smell that clings to John when he comes from the firehouse in the wee hours. But on those nights, the scent is comforting, seeping into her sleep and alerting her that her husband is back safe and sound for another night, another day.

Missing her husband desperately, J.J. fights back tears and beats a staccato on the armrest with fingertips that have been chewed raw.

I can't do this. I can't.

A panic attack can trigger your fight-or-flight instinct, Dr. Michaels had told her. *When that happens, try to remember that most likely, the perception of danger isn't grounded in reality. Use your breathing exercises to control your anxiety.*

Sometimes that works. Not today. Those fires are definitely real.

She grabs her bag and digs through it, past the clutter she never unpacked from last week's trip and cigarettes she can't smoke and the antianxiety medication that failed to ease her anxiety.

She finds her phone and pulls up John's number. His voice will ground her. It always does.

But when she presses the icon to send the call, nothing happens.

She tries again. Nothing.

The phone is an old model, and she'd figured it would stop working one day, but did it have to be this one?

She tosses the phone onto the seat with an exasperated grunt.

The driver flicks his attention to the rearview mirror, then reaches back to slide open the divider. "Everything okay?"

"I'm trying to make a call, but it won't go through."

"How many bars do you have?"

"Bars?"

"Signal strength."

"Oh! I didn't even think of that." She checks the phone. "I don't see any bars."

"Then there's no signal. Digital service can be intermittent around here on a good day. With the fires, anything can happen. The cell towers might be compromised, or there might be power outages . . . sometimes, in weather like this, it's for public safety."

"What do you mean?"

"They'll deliberately cut the power to help contain the fires. That might be what happened."

Terrific.

She thanks him and closes the divider, jarred by the realization that she's all alone in the world. Yes, the driver is here, but he's a stranger, and her friends are waiting, but—

As she puts the phone back into her bag, her fingers graze the pack of cigarettes. She hesitates, then pulls it out and looks for her lighter. It seems to have disappeared. She dumps the contents of the bag into her lap, ignoring several items that fall to the floor as she searches the heap.

No lighter.

Maybe she lost it. Or maybe it had been confiscated by airport security when she sent the bag through the carry-on X-ray machine.

She repacks the bag and bends over to retrieve the rest of her belongings from the floor. Ballpoint pen, face mask, orange prescription bottle . . .

Too bad it's too soon for another dose.

About to put it back into her bag, she pauses. Had she swallowed one pill, or two, in the car with the champagne? Or, wait a minute . . .

Had she taken it at all? Maybe she hadn't.

Maybe she'd considered it and then forgotten, discombobulated from the travel flurry and not being able to sneak a smoke between the plane and the car.

She must not have taken it. That would explain why it isn't working.

She opens the bottle, shakes a couple of capsules into her palm, pops them into her mouth.

Her mouth is dry, and the pills lodge in her throat.

At last she forces them down, biting her lips together to keep from gagging. Her teeth dig into her lip and the mineral tang of blood taints her mouth as she leans back and closes her eyes, longing for John, for their son, for home . . .

She shouldn't have come, but there's no going back now. She's trapped.

It's the same thought she'd had as an eighteen-year-old freshman embarking on her first semester at Northwestern University, hurtling toward the new life waiting whether she was ready or not.

Then, as now, she was leaving behind a familiar existence, terrified to be striking out on her own. Then, as now, she assured herself that it was a positive change, and things could only get better.

Then, she'd believed it.

And now?

J.J. considers the past—distant, and recent. And the future.

She thinks about all the things this vast fortune will change.

About all the things that no amount of money can ever change.

LEILA

After showing Leila around and escorting her to a luxurious second-floor suite, Shea Daniels's assistant, Justin, left her to her own devices. Unfortunately, her devices—the electronic ones—are no longer functioning.

Service had been sketchy on the way up the coast, but she'd had two bars when she arrived an hour ago. She'd texted Molly and J.J., opting to ignore several angry messages from her daughters and her boss.

She'd quit her job last night via an email to HR, offering no notice or explanation and feeling no regret over burning that bridge.

Then she'd phoned her ex-husband to say she'd been called out of town on business.

"But you were just away last weekend!"

"That wasn't business, Warren. And you still owe me from last March when you couldn't see them for two weeks."

"I couldn't help that. I was sick, and then Nicole got sick, and then the boys . . ."

The boys.

Every time he uses the phrase, Leila finds herself bristling. Warren is a self-described guy's guy, and had been hoping for a boy with both Leila's pregnancies. Now he has two: a toddler with his second wife, and a thirteen-year-old stepson from her first marriage.

"I understand," she said. "And I can't help this."

"I know, it's just . . . We have dinner plans for Saturday night."

"The girls don't need a babysitter, Warren. You and Nicole can go out to dinner."

"It's not . . . it's . . . the boys are coming, too. There's a new hibachi place we've all been wanting to try, and we finally got a reservation."

Leila got the message loud and clear—it's family night, not date night. New family only.

"Sorry to put a crimp in your plans, Warren, but I have to go away, so the girls have to stay."

"What about Gib? Isn't he going to be around?"

"No," she lied.

The conversation hadn't ended pleasantly. No surprise that Warren hadn't exactly smoothed things over with Kate and Ellie on her behalf. They're furious about being stuck in Orange County for the weekend.

It's probably just as well that she's out of touch with them. She would, however, like an update from Molly and J.J. And she does wonder whether anyone else might be trying to get in touch with her.

Specifically . . . Stef.

On the heels of quitting her job and arguing with

Warren and the girls, she'd done something reckless. Stupid, even.

Yes, she, Leila—who'd convinced Molly not to reveal their lottery win to her own mother—had shared the news about the win *and* the weekend trip with her married lover.

Former lover.

Of course, Stef isn't just *anyone*. Their relationship goes back to their college days, when he'd lived across the hall.

And Stef was Molly's boyfriend before Leila took up with him. Well, *when* Leila took up with him.

Back in college, it had only been that one time. She hated herself afterward, even before Molly found out. Miraculously, their friendship survived. Most importantly, hers with Molly. But also hers with Stef; even, eventually, Molly's with Stef.

It had taken years for Leila to recognize that first ill-fated fling with an off-limits man as a pattern.

Warren had been engaged to someone else when they met.

And Stef, the second time around—Stef was married to someone else. *Is* married. Intends to *stay* married.

Or so he told Leila when their affair began last fall, and again last spring when she ended it. His wife is the executive VP of marketing at a major corporation. He'd left his sales job when their first child was born and was a stay-at-home dad until their fourth started school a few years ago. Like Warren, like most men, Stef had navigated reentry without a hitch, and his career is back on the upswing. He isn't interested in risking custody of his kids, or moving out of his lavish Escondido home, or losing the extravagant life-style his wife's money provides—exotic travels, even a yacht.

But now that there's been a cataclysmic shift in Leila's status, he wouldn't have to.

That's what she wanted him to know.

So she'd texted him, asking him to please call her. If he hadn't, she would have let it go, because after spontaneously reaching out, she'd realized it was a mistake and hoped that he wouldn't call.

But he had.

She led off with the bombshell. As he digested the news in stunned silence, she just kept on talking, talking, talking—her usual coping strategy whenever she senses that she's not going to hear what she wants to hear. Sometimes it works—with Gib, Warren, her daughters, her friends.

With Stef, she'd prattled on about Shea and the week-end at Windfall, and she'd promised that she'd hire him the best lawyer in the world so that he wouldn't lose anything in a divorce, and she'd told him that this ticket was *their* ticket—to a fresh start, together, because her wealth would change everything for her, for *them*, and . . . and . . . and—

"Leila, stop!" he finally cut in. "I can't even think! I need to think."

"Think about what?"

"I just . . . I don't know."

"What don't you know? You don't know what you need to think about?"

"I don't know if this is what I want."

Translation: *I don't know if I want you.*

Rather: *I don't want you.*

Because if you want someone, and they want you, you don't need to think about anything. You just need to plan, and do.

That's fine. She doesn't need him, or any man. Not anymore. Finally, finally, she's completely self-sufficient. It's time for *her* to start thinking. About the future, and where she wants to live, and where she wants to travel, and what she wants to buy.

And if she could get online right now, she could start planning and doing.

Justin had given her a thick packet of papers, including Wi-Fi information and a password, but the network isn't even showing up in her settings. Hoping it's a temporary glitch, she goes through the rest of the information.

A black folder engraved *Windfall* in gold script is filled with documents and forms. There's a full itinerary that begins with a champagne celebration this afternoon. There's a full slate of meetings tomorrow with the professionals on Shea's team whose headshots and impressive biographies are attached. There are menus, too, for gourmet dinners that will be delivered each evening.

She pockets her phone and steps into the cavernous corridor, dimly lit with wall sconces and lined with closed doors. Shorter hallways branch off toward the back of the house at either end of the hall, with the grand stairway in the middle. There, a wide flight leads to the first floor, and a narrower one continues up to the third.

Earlier, she'd sworn she'd heard footsteps moving about overhead. Thinking it might be one of her friends, she'd called their names from the foot of the steps.

Justin heard her and materialized in the entryway below. "They're not here yet, but I'm watching for them from the front parlor. I'll let you know."

"Oh . . . I thought I heard someone on the third floor."

"Must have been the wind. There's nothing up there but Shea's suite, really, and storage, and you and I are the only ones here."

It hadn't been the wind. The wind doesn't sound like footsteps.

She glances back at the third-floor stairway as she descends quickly to the first, gripping the wrought-iron railing. The cavernous foyer is dimly lit by an antique fixture high overhead. Beyond the curved archway into the front parlor, she can see Justin napping in a chair facing the window.

He reminds her of a preternaturally preserved leading man; one of those people whose age is difficult to guess. He appears to have had some cosmetic work done, and his hair is too thick and blond to be natural unless he's around Leila's age. Even then, a stretch.

During the pandemic lockdown, she'd discovered that she had far more gray hair than the few strands that had caused her to start coloring it in her early thirties. She got her hands on a home dye kit and started doing it herself—well, with some help from her daughters, back when they still liked her. It was darker and more one-dimensional, but it would have to do. By the time salons reopened, her business was failing and she couldn't afford even a pedicure, much less custom color with highlights or lowlights.

Now, though . . .

Now she'll become a regular at one of those high-end places in Beverly Hills, where beauty—along with eternal youth—can be bought, if you have enough money. She will always, always have enough money, for everything she could ever dream of.

She moves on through the house. It's grand but not formal, with terrazzo floors and exposed beams, exterior doors opening onto gardens and terraces. Most rooms have cozy seating areas and tile fireplaces with slate mantels and ornate wrought-iron grillwork.

It's all too easy to imagine Chantal Charbonneau here.

The place doesn't appear to have changed much in the last twenty years or even in the last hundred. There are no televisions, computers, or air conditioners. The furniture is antique. The built-in bookcases are lined with leather-bound classics. The bathrooms have claw-foot tubs and pull-chain toilets.

Despite the vintage setting, the past might not seem to lurk so palpably in every room if Leila hadn't done her homework last night, reading about Windfall's storied past and a long line of ill-fated former residents before Chantal Charbonneau.

Wandering through the rooms, she hears phantom tunes tinkling from a player piano, glimpses a woman in a lace dress amid fluttering lace curtains, smells French cologne mingling with the faint scent of wildfire drifting through the open windows. The air is warm, yet she's chilled through, feeling uncomfortably alone.

"There's no staff on the premises when clients are here, to ensure their utmost privacy," Justin had informed her. "And of course, for safety reasons, no electronic surveillance . . . cameras, that sort of thing."

"Isn't a lack of security the opposite of safe?"

"Ah, I said lack of electronic surveillance—not the same thing as a lack of security. Shea will tell you more when she gets here a little later today. Now let me show you where to find a snack in case you're hungry . . ."

She wasn't then, but now she's famished, and dinner delivery isn't until late this evening. She makes her way to the huge kitchen, with its dark cabinetry, Spanish tile, and a massive hood above a six-burner restaurant-style stove.

A bottle of Louis Roederer Cristal is chilling in a glass bucket on the white marble counter. A silver tray holds three crystal flutes, a bowl of deep red, unblemished strawberries, and the largest box of gourmet chocolates Leila has ever seen.

Justin had told her to help herself, but she leaves the spread untouched. J.J. and Molly should get the full effect, to help dispel any doubts they might have about being here.

She grabs a protein bar from a glass jar on the breakfast bar and opens the fridge. It's wood-paneled, built into the wall, and twice as wide as hers back home. The brightly lit glass shelves are lined with food and beverages, drawers filled with fresh fruits and vegetables. She grabs a water bottle and some fruit, exiting the kitchen with one last glance at the spread on the counter.

Any minute. Molly and J.J. will be here any minute, and then the three of them will pop that cork and celebrate.

Pocketing the protein bar and biting into her apple, she spies an old-fashioned wall phone and hurries over to lift the receiver, connected to the base by a spiral cord. There's no dial tone. She hadn't really expected one.

It's been years since she dialed a landline, and the only number she knows by heart these days is for her childhood home. Everyone else—everyone who matters—is programmed in her cell phone.

She checks again. Still no messages, still no service.

She steps outside, moving away from the house along a stone walkway. It winds past gardens, tennis courts, and a large swimming pool that looks inviting right about now, with the excessive midday heat untempered by strong Santa Ana winds.

Classic fire weather.

She looks back toward the burning hills, obstructed by what seems like a thicker haze than when she first got here. Pausing to sip some water, she checks again for a signal—nope—before moving on, toward the ocean and open space.

She follows a seaside trail toward the property's highest point, treading slowly and carefully, aware not just of the poor air quality but of the thin perimeter separating path from drop-off. She's winded when she reaches the promontory, where a weathered wooden platform holds a couple of Adirondack chairs that face the water.

It would be a spectacular spot to watch a Pacific sunset if the sun and sea weren't shrouded by smoke.

She steps as close as she dares to the edge of the cliff and tosses the apple core over. She can see scrubby branches jutting from crags in the rock just below, far too flimsy to break a fall. Stepping back toward the platform with a shudder, she spots a white stone marker and leans in to read the inscription.

He who has gone, so we but cherish his memory, abides with us, more potent, nay, more present than the living man.

—ANTOINE DE SAINT-EXUPÉRY

This must be the spot from which Chantal Charbonneau was believed to have jumped, or been pushed, or fallen.

Of the three options, the last seems most believable. If she'd come out here alone and lost her footing, she'd have landed on jagged boulders and been swallowed by crashing surf far below.

She wonders who'd placed the marker.

The quote isn't familiar, but Antoine de Saint-Exupéry . . .

She can't place the name, oddly familiar. Someone had mentioned him recently, but she can't place the details. Snapping a photo of the quote with her phone as a reminder, she notes that service bars have appeared at last.

She checks her texts.

Stef has not suddenly materialized, as she had known he would not, despite an irrational fleeting notion that he's suddenly psychic.

There's nothing more from the girls, Warren, Gib . . .

That gives her pause. He isn't much of a phone person. Particularly not in the midst of a busy day on campus. Still, he could have checked to see if she'd arrived and how things were going.

Though if he had, she wouldn't have seen it until now, and anyway, things had shifted between them before she left. Mostly on her end, lingering resentment over his accusation that she's controlling, along with the knowledge that she's completely self-sufficient at last. But she senses a shift on his end, too. Maybe he's worried that she'll move on now that she doesn't need his roof over her head, or maybe he's rethinking his stance on marriage.

She only knows that their interaction last night and this morning had felt subdued, and she was relieved when her driver pulled up just before Gib was going to leave for campus. For some reason, she took satisfaction in being the first to leave, waving at him standing by his beat-up Subaru as she was swept away to Windfall.

She sends a new message on the group text to her friends: **Checking in on your ETA?**

Waiting for a response, she stares at the stone marker in memory of the woman who'd once inhabited this very spot.

How Chantal must have savored the solitude at Windfall after her years in the limelight's glare, hounded by the press, smothered by obligations, surrounded by people who only wanted something from her.

Yeah. Leila gets it. Gets Chantal, gets the overwhelming urge to escape.

As soon as she gets the money, she's going to get the hell out of LA and find a magnificent house on a large piece of property. Maybe even right here along the Central Coast . . .

Though, Gib won't want to make the commute.

And the girls will complain—about being isolated, and about being even farther than Anaheim is from school and their friends.

Maybe they'll decide to move in with Warren full-time. Maybe Leila will agree to that.

Maybe Gib will opt to stay in Reseda. Maybe Leila won't mind being single again.

Maybe it's what she needs, after wasting so many years on endless responsibilities and relationships with people who profess to love her only to hurt her, time and again.

Maybe there's a reason she's the kind of person who lets go. Maybe it's because others have let her go, have let her down, from the moment she was born.

She imagines herself all alone, making a fresh start just as she had when she'd moved to LA after college. Alone . . . but powerless no more.

MOLLY

Friday evening, Molly sets her hair on hot rollers, refreshes her makeup, and dresses for dinner in a pink silk pantsuit she'd chosen back home from a closet full of pretty clothes she hasn't even thought about since before she had Dawson. It seems two sizes smaller than the last time she wore it, as do the spectator pumps she manages to wedge her feet into. But this is the fanciest outfit she brought with her, and fancy is in order, based on the setting and the menu and all she's experienced here so far.

She, Leila, and J.J. had enjoyed a champagne toast this afternoon—just the three of them, plus Dawson, of course. The bubbly brought on a pleasant blur, filled with hugs and giddy laughter and lots of toasts.

Afterward, Molly returned to her suite, put the baby down for a nap, and promptly drifted off herself. She'd awakened to dusk, a day-drinking hangover, and a room that feels close and stuffy, probably because she's so accustomed to air-conditioning.

The accommodations are otherwise perfect. The suite

is decorated in shades of white and buttery cream, with mahogany furniture and luxurious linens. On one wall, tall windows overlook a bougainvillea-filled courtyard with a splashing fountain. On another, arched French doors lead to a wide, shaded balcony. The adjacent dressing room has been made over into a nursery stocked with everything a traveling baby might need.

She fed Dawson and gave him a bottle, hoping he'll allow her to enjoy dinner and regretting, yet again, that she hadn't left him behind with her parents.

Her mom might be worried by now, though Molly had answered her daily text upon landing in LA, saying all is well and that it's a busy day—the truth.

Unfortunately, cell service is still unavailable here, though Leila had mentioned she'd been able to get a signal out by the water.

Maybe they can go out there after dinner. She'll need to come up with some excuse for missing the family barbecue tomorrow. A white lie, as Leila would call it. But for Molly, a lie is a lie.

She grabs a sweater for Dawson, putting it into the diaper bag along with extra food, toys, a teething ring, and pacifier.

"You're going to be a good boy for Mama tonight, aren't you?"

He's lying on his back in the center of the bed, bicycling his little legs and making contented noises, a stream of saliva trickling from his gummy grin. She buries her face in his chubby belly, blowing raspberries, and he laughs out loud.

"You beautiful, beautiful boy. I love you so much, yes, I do, yes I do."

She picks him up and checks the itinerary, then the mantel clock.

Cocktail hour begins in fifteen minutes. She'll head down in five.

Her eye goes to the oil painting above the fireplace: a lonely figure silhouetted on a cliff above the sea.

Is the artwork original to the house? Was it here when Chantal Charbonneau lived here? Had she bought or commissioned the piece, maybe seeing her own sense of isolation reflected in the stark image? Or had it come after she'd gone, meant to depict the actor herself, just before she jumped—or was pushed—to her death?

Or ran off to reinvent herself, according to Leila's theory.

Molly thinks again of the shadowy figure she'd seen— well, thought she'd seen—watching from the cupola as she arrived. What if Chantal's ghost isn't merely haunting this place; what if Chantal is still here—alive? What if—

Molly quickly turns away from the painting and opens one of the French doors. The breeze is warmer than the room, and smells of wildfire.

She steps onto the balcony. It runs the width of the house and down along the two shorter perpendicular wings. Stairways on either end lead to an enclosed courtyard bordered by the house on three sides. On the fourth, red bougainvillea cascades over a wrought-iron fence with a gate. There are several loungers, tables, a fountain, and tall succulents growing in Mexican pottery.

On a nice day, it would be an inviting place to relax, but not today. Earlier, Leila had assured her that heat and wind and smoke are to be expected in fire season. She would know, after two decades in California, and she didn't seem particularly fazed by it. J.J., though . . . J.J. seemed uneasy, too.

Dawson's drool-drenched fingers find a clump of her wind-whipped hair. She winces, trying to untangle it. "Ouch, sweetie. That hurts Mama. Please don't—"

She breaks off, spotting Leila as she steps through the gate into the courtyard. She's walking briskly, phone in hand.

Molly opens her mouth to call out to her, then sees the expression on Leila's face and thinks better of it.

She's clearly upset about something. Certain she'll fill them all in at dinner, Molly slips back inside.

SHEA

Shea dresses as she would for any other meet-the-new-clients dinner, in a sleeveless black sheath, pumps, and pearls. She's wearing a bit of makeup and her long, dark hair twisted into a sleek chignon.

Inspecting her reflection in her full-length dressing room mirror, she resists the urge to add some eyeliner and perhaps some red lipstick instead of nude gloss. Understated, professional elegance is the goal, not . . .

No. Not that. Not Beck.

When she got here, Justin informed her that all the clients were settled in. Beck, Elizabeth, and Morgan had yet to arrive.

After sending Justin on his way, she'd retreated to her third-floor suite, hoping to check in on Abi and his family and catch up on calls and emails. Unfortunately, telecommunications have been disrupted by the wildfires. This isn't the first time that's happened here, and there's no way of knowing how long it will last. Having tuned in to the local news on the car radio earlier, she knows only that the fire is contained. That's reassuring, though contained doesn't mean extinguished.

Her suite encompasses half the third floor, with views to the north, west, and south. To see the east, where the fire is burning, she has to go to the top of the house.

She steps out into the hallway and walks past closed doors to vacant rooms, opening the one that leads to a narrow staircase. She flips a switch and a bare bulb illuminates the steep flight to the cupola.

She smells a faint whiff of tobacco in the air as she ascends, and remembers Chantal, puffing menthol from a long-handled gold Tiffany cigarette holder.

Perched atop the red tile roof, the cupola has windows on all four walls. Dust floats in the glow from the bare bulb overhead. A thick layer of it covers the old plank floor, along with mouse droppings.

The eaves and woodwork are draped in cobwebs and spiderwebs—which are not the same thing, she'd learned on a long-ago day when she and Corey ducked into the shed to escape the rain.

"I'm afraid of spiders!" Shea had said, cowering in the doorway.

"Why? Spiders are amazing. I've got a book about them. I'll show you when we get home. Now come on, you're getting soaked."

"No! It's too scary!"

"But you're strong and brave."

"Not when there are cobwebs!"

"Don't worry, sweetie. Cobwebs aren't spiderwebs. They

used to be, but they don't have spiders in them anymore. The spiders leave them behind and move on. They're like empty houses. You're not afraid of houses, are you?"

Back then, she was afraid of everything.

Now she's afraid of nothing.

When the most terrifying nightmares you ever imagined have come to fruition, there's nothing left to fear.

She crosses the room. There are windows on all four walls—a waste of spectacular vista, in Shea's opinion, as this is designated storage space. There's not much to store: boxes of DVDs and CDs and the defunct electronic devices that go with them; a few plastic tubs filled with childhood mementos; and several old wooden interior doors with vintage hardware.

A telescope is positioned in the western window—a remnant from Chantal's residency, untouched throughout Shea's. She glances at it, then does a double take.

Something isn't right. It's been moved.

Walking toward it, she notes that the dust is disturbed in her path, and that a large cobweb that had been strung from the scope to the tripod has been broken. Make that a spiderweb, its industrious owner busily weaving delicate strands back into place.

They do that, Shea recalls, according to that book of Corey's. If an orb web is partially broken, a spider will very quickly repair it.

She removes the lens cap carefully, so as not to change the angle of the scope, and leans in to look. It's focused on the sea, same as always—but not just at the open water, where at this time of year you can spot blue whales and humpbacks. No, now it's trained on the property's highest spot—the platform with the Adirondack chairs and the stone marker in memory of Chantal.

Someone moved the telescope in her absence.

Her gaze falls on the spider, busily repairing its recently torn web.

Today. Nobody would have had any reason to be up here today.

But somebody was.

J.J.

The library, where predinner drinks are to be served, is a cozy first-floor room with leather furniture and floor-to-ceiling bookshelves and a fully stocked wet bar.

J.J. finds Molly already there, seated on a sofa with a glass of white wine, with Dawson beside her in his carrier. Her face is made up, her blond hair falls past her shoulder in shiny waves, and she's wearing a fancy pink outfit.

"Crap! I knew I packed all wrong," J.J. says, gesturing at her blouse, khaki skirt, and loafers. "Wait, that's a lie. I didn't pack wrong. I just don't own anything nice enough for this place."

"Don't be silly. You look fine, and it's just us."

"What about Shea and her team?"

"Well, us and them. But we're just staying here, so . . . it's not like you have to be all dressed up."

"*You* are."

"This suit is old and out of style, and there's already a drool stain on my shoulder, and the waistband is a tourniquet. But that's okay . . . we'll both get whole new wardrobes. Won't that be a blast?"

"Well . . . shopping has never been my thing, so . . ."

"It's always been *my* thing, so I'll help you. Just like back in college. Remember? When we went to every store on Michigan Avenue looking for outfits to wear for that rush party?"

"Oh, I remember. You were the best personal shopper ever, although it didn't do me much good, did it? I didn't get a single bid."

"Well, Leila didn't get any she wanted."

"She wasn't into it any more than I was, though. You were the only sorority girl in our group, Molly."

"Thank goodness it only took me one semester to figure out that my so-called sisters were just an organized band of mean girls. I'm so glad I never— Oh, hey, Leila."

J.J. turns to see her in the doorway, wearing a blue dress with a deep V neckline that accentuates her gold sapphire necklace.

"Is everything okay?" Molly asks her.

"Yes. Why?"

"No reason. You just seem a little . . ."

Leila frowns and looks at J.J., who shrugs, not sure what Molly's talking about. Leila seems like her usual self, briskly crossing to the vintage cocktail cart and surveying the row of bottles.

"Who wants a drink?"

"I've already got mine." Molly holds up her wineglass.

"You and your pinot grigio. J.J.? Gin and tonic?"

"No, thanks. I promised myself I wouldn't drink tonight."

"Oh, please. My whole life is about broken promises—especially to myself—and compromises. And about being overworked and overtired, underpaid and underfed. There's never enough. Not enough time, or money, or . . . me. I'm just . . . never enough."

Leila's words resonate. J.J. nods. "I feel the same way."

"So do I," Molly agrees. "My mom would probably say the same thing. My sisters, too."

"A lot of women would. Women are the ones who, if they want to have it all, are expected to put their lives on hold for pregnancy." Leila grabs two glasses and starts plunking ice cubes into them, one at a time, as if punctuating her points. "And then women are expected to pick up their careers where they left off without missing a beat."

Plunk. Plunk.

"And everything changes in their absence—their old networking contacts have moved on, or the whole world has gone digital, or whatever, and everything they knew how to do is done differently now, and their experience is no longer relevant."

Plunk.

"Leila," J.J. attempts to cut in.

"And then . . . and *then*, when a woman *finally* gets someone to hire her and give her a chance . . ." *plunk* ". . . the job doesn't even align with her education and skill set and track record. And she has to work so much harder for so much less. And she'll never—"

"Wait, Leila!"

"What?" The plunking stops, and she looks up at J.J.

"I really can't."

"Oh, come on. One won't hurt." Leila pours a healthy portion of Hendrick's into each glass.

"It might. You're not supposed to mix the grain and the grape, and I've had a lot of *grape* today."

Leila waves her off. "The champagne was hours ago."

"Well, you're not supposed to mix my medication with alcohol, either, so I'd better stick with club soda."

"Wait, what medication? Are you sick?" Molly's hand goes to Dawson's carrier handle as if she wants to move him out of germ range.

"Don't worry, I'm not contagious. It's for sleep. I have insomnia. You know that, Leila. Remember? We talked about it. At Christmas."

Leila looks puzzled.

"Remember? You called me to catch up right before the holidays."

Leila shrugs. Clearly, the memory is lost to her, but it's indelible in J.J.'s brain.

They'd chatted for almost an hour that night, about everything from work to their families to insomnia.

"I have it, too. I've had it for years," she had told J.J. in that familiar one-upmanship tone. "Have you tried sleeping pills?"

"Yes, but I'm not supposed to take them every night and when I don't, I can't sleep."

"Then you should take them every night. How about your phone? Do you have it auto-set for Do Not Disturb when you go to bed?"

"I can't do that with Brian deployed. What if something happens?"

"Nothing's going to happen, and even if it did, the military doesn't call or text you in the middle of the night," Leila had said as if she knew, because Leila thought she knew everything. "Anyway, if they couldn't get ahold of you, they'd call John."

"But John works the overnight shift, and he wouldn't be able to call me."

"Sure he would. You set it up so that certain numbers can get through. I'll show you how to do it."

"I don't know . . ."

"J.J., electronics mess with sleep patterns. I'll send you an article about it. Screens interfere with the surge of melatonin we need to fall asleep. You can google it."

J.J. had, of course, as soon as they hung up. Turned out Leila was right.

So she tried it. She put her phone on Do Not Disturb mode, set so that she could still receive incoming calls and texts from John and Brian. That night, she'd slept better than she had in months, and she texted Leila in the morning to thank her.

Leila, apparently, has forgotten the whole thing.

She adds a splash of tonic to the drinks. "Listen, J.J., most prescription labels have that alcohol warning, but believe me, you'll be fine."

"Thank you, Dr. Randolph, but I'd rather not—"

"Hey, I *was* premed, J.J. How many times do I have to tell you, it's not like you're downing a fistful of pills with a fifth of vodka."

J.J. stiffens. "Leila, that's—"

"Hey!" Leila takes a closer look at her, then turns a probing gaze on Molly. "Where are your September Girls necklaces? We said we'd all wear them this weekend! Didn't you two bring yours?"

"I did, but this guy is a handful," Molly says, gesturing at Dawson. "Y'all are lucky I managed to put clothes on."

"Same here. I mean, not because of the baby," J.J. adds, "but I was wiped out even before all the travel and champagne."

"Then you definitely won't need sleeping pills tonight." Leila twists lime wedges into the drinks.

J.J. opens her mouth to explain that she's on other medication, too, but thinks better of it. Her friends don't know about the anxiety and depression, and, anyway, does she really want to get into that discussion *now*?

No. She does not.

Really, all she wants right now is John—even just hearing his voice would help, but her phone isn't working.

She also wants nicotine. Earlier, she'd found a book of matches in a kitchen drawer and snuck a couple of cigarettes upstairs in her room. She'd felt like a kid again, standing in front of the open window, blowing tobacco smoke into the smokier air outside.

If only she could go back to her room right now to relax with a cigarette.

A book, too. Preferably one she's already read. She stares at the wall of shelves behind her, lined with row upon row of titles she remembers from English lit, like old friends waiting to embrace her and carry her back to a familiar place.

Leila hands J.J. a glass and clinks it with her own, then clinks Molly's. "To the September Girls."

"To the September Girls," J.J. says, forcing a smile and taking a sip.

LEILA

Broken promises . . . compromises. . . .

That Molly and J.J. can relate to Leila's life experience probably shouldn't have surprised her, but it had. Pleasantly. Because although she sometimes feels as though life has swept them in such different directions that they share little common ground, that isn't the case.

Work hard, earn reward—such a simple premise. They'd all spent their formative years trying to achieve academic status to gain admission to the right university that would lead to a successful career and financial stability, yet somehow, things hadn't turned out that way for any of them. Disillusionment and deprivation are so ingrained at this point that it's hard to flip a switch and change that mindset.

But this weekend is about letting go and moving on, about celebrating a much brighter future.

It's certainly not about venturing back out into the smoky evening to the cliffside spot where her phone gets a signal to see if Stef has responded to her most recent text, consisting of a single straightforward word: **Well?**

She'd also messaged Gib, letting him know that phone service is sketchy and she'll be out of touch, though she hadn't heard from him, either.

However, with school dismissed for the day, there are a barrage of texts and missed calls from her daughters. They're still begging her to cut short her trip and rescue them from Anaheim.

Not an option, sorry, she replied on a group text, then deleted the *sorry*, hit Send, and walked away.

Settling on the couch beside Molly, she glances down at Dawson, remembering her own daughters at that age, so sweetly content. She never would have imagined that they'd grow into self-centered, entitled teenagers.

Dawson shakes his wooden rattle, then flings it across the floor.

"Whoopsie!" Leila grabs it and returns it to his chubby fist.

Delighted, he tosses the rattle again. This time, it lands at J.J.'s feet.

"Whoopsie!" She, too, takes up the game with a grin, handing it back to him.

"Y'all, don't encourage him! He's just going to— See?" Molly shakes her head as Dawson throws the toy once more.

"Whoopsie!" Leila scoops it up and hands it back. "You silly guy!"

The rattle sails from his grasp once more, but this time, Molly catches it. "Dawson, no. Let Auntie Leila and Auntie J.J. relax now."

He starts to emit an impatient protest, but it's curtailed when she hands him a cloth book with crinkly pages that instantly captivate him.

"Thanks, guys," Molly says. "It's sweet of you to put up with him."

"Put up with him? Don't be silly. He's adorable."

"He really is, Mol. So precious," J.J. agrees, settling into a wingback chair, already making short work of the drink she'd said she didn't want.

Leila's is going down quickly as well, not just because she's thirsty in this heat. All that tension she'd carried back from the water's edge, wrapped up in texts and calls she had—and hadn't—received . . .

It's oozing away on a warm ripple of gin.

"I meant to ask you earlier, Leila, about the ticket," J.J. says.

"What about it?"

"How'd it go at the bank?"

"Fine. Why?"

"I just wanted to make sure there were no surprises."

Is it Leila's imagination, or is J.J. suspicious?

"What kind of surprises?"

"You don't think anyone saw the ticket? When you put it into the box?"

"Of course nobody saw." She drains her glass and stands. "Who's ready for another round?"

"I am," Molly says.

J.J. shrugs. "Why not."

Leila busies herself at the cocktail cart, pouring wine, mixing drinks, assuring herself that everything between the three of them is the same as always.

But when Molly says, "I feel like y'all understand how special he is to me," Leila is certain for a wild moment that she's read Leila's mind and is talking about Stef; that she knows, and J.J. knows, and—

But no, Molly is referring to Dawson, now cuddled on her lap sucking on a bottle.

"Of course, we understand," J.J. assures her.

"Yeah, we're moms, too, remember?" Leila hands her a full wineglass, delivers one gin and tonic to J.J., and returns to her seat with the other.

"My sisters are moms, too," Molly is saying, "and I mean, they try, you know? But with them, Dawson's just one more kid in the cousins mix. Y'all are different, even though you've already been there, done that."

"It's nice to spend time with a baby again," Leila assures her. "Babies are so much easier than teenagers. Especially mine."

"Aw, honey, all teenage girls are hard. Believe me, I get it. There were five of us in my house, growing up."

"Well, I don't know how your mother kept her sanity. I keep questioning myself, wondering what I could have done to make things better with my girls—to make *them* better. Because they're just . . ."

"Leila! You're fine. I'm sure they're fine," Molly says. "It's just a phase. They'll grow out of it."

"What if they don't?"

"Maybe they won't," J.J. tells her, "but you shouldn't blame yourself."

"Well, as much as I'd love to think this is all Warren's fault, I've always been the primary parent."

"But you have joint custody," Molly protests.

"I've made so many mistakes, though, as a mother. And I feel like it's the one thing in life you can't afford to get wrong, you know? You can change careers, you can change who you're married to or even whether you're married, but being a parent . . . once you're in, you're in, you know?"

J.J. nods. "I never thought of it that way, but it's true."

"But, Leila, you didn't get it wrong," Molly says. "You were the one who was there for your girls while their dad was off starting a new life with some other woman."

"I still missed a lot. I was so preoccupied with trying to get my business off the ground."

"Every working mother has to deal with that," J.J. comments.

"But I did it all for nothing. I was so sure my boutique was going to be a huge success—I envisioned it as this flagship store for a retail brand that was going to take over the world. That's why I called it *Leila*. It was all mine, and I was going to prove to everyone that I have what it takes to be a success, and I was going to be such a great role model for my girls. Instead, I'm a failure."

"Oh, Leila, you are not," Molly says. "The pandemic destroyed a lot of businesses."

"And then there's the pandemic. Overnight the girls

and I went from hardly seeing each other to being together 24-7. I was way too hard on them during the lockdown."

"Everyone went through that, though."

Leila sighs. She isn't sure what the point even is, but there's something cathartic about unburdening herself on two people who love her despite her flaws. Then again, they were questioning her about the bank as if they don't trust her.

"What if this is just who my daughters are? What am I even supposed to do about it? I can't change what happened. I can't change them. Can't make them less selfish, make them care about other people, or—"

"Leila! Stop," Molly says. "You're a great mom."

"I'm definitely not a great mom."

"I'm sure you were the best mom you could be under the circumstances."

"I wasn't." Seeing Molly's troubled expression, she shifts gears. "But hey, I always heard that boys are easier, so I'm sure *you* won't go through this. J.J. didn't, right, J.J.?"

"Boys come with a whole different set of issues. Or at least, my son did. Brian always kept everything inside. I never knew what he was thinking, about anything."

"I *wish* I didn't know what my girls were thinking. Anyway, J.J., that's not necessarily a boy thing. It's a *you* thing. You've always been introspective, and so is John, from what I remember," Leila adds, having only met J.J.'s husband a couple of times, and years ago.

J.J. shakes her head, staring down into her glass as if she didn't hear. "I should never have allowed him to meet with that damned recruiter."

"Brian?" Molly asks.

"Yes. As soon as he heard they'd pay full tuition after active duty, he was sold. If we could have afforded to send him to college, he wouldn't be . . ." She clears her throat hard and swallows some gin.

"Brian's doing such a noble thing, honey," Molly says. "You should be so proud of him for stepping up to serve his country."

"But the *Marines*? I should have talked him into something safer. Some other military branch."

"There's risk in every branch," Leila says. "It's what he wanted to do. You couldn't stop him. He's a grown man."

Molly chimes in, "And really, there's risk everywhere. I mean, John's a firefighter, so you're used to—"

"This isn't about John, okay?"

"I'm sorry, J.J. I didn't mean to . . ." Molly shakes her head. "I'm really sorry."

"It's just . . . your child is your child, no matter how old he is. You'll understand someday, Molly. Don't ever let anything happen to your son. You have to protect him. Keep him close to you."

"I try. That's why he's here. It was hard enough to be away from him last weekend. I can't imagine how I'd feel if he was on the other side of the world right now."

Again, J.J. stares down into her drink.

Molly catches Leila's eye, as if to say, *Fix this.*

"You know how I'd feel if my girls were on the other side of the world?" Leila hears herself say. "Elated."

"Leila!" Molly's brows disappear beneath her bangs.

But she talks on, telling them all about her daughters—how they constantly bicker with each other and with her, doing an imitation of a put-out teenage girl that soon has them both laughing.

She can feel the gin making its way from her empty stomach to her head, loosening her tongue on the way.

"I know this sounds terrible, but I guess I kind of understand now why she just let me go, you know?"

"Who?" J.J. asks.

"My mother."

"Your birth mother?"

"No! My adoptive mother. I used to wonder why she didn't make more effort to get me back after I dropped out of premed . . . not that it would have worked. But still . . ."

"She did try, Leila. I remember her calling, and asking to speak to you, and you wouldn't take the calls. Remember that, J.J.?"

"Yes. I remember."

"Well, I always thought it would have been nice if she'd tried a little harder."

"She might have, eventually. If she'd lived long enough. I feel like your father and brothers deserve a lot more of the blame in this."

"But they're men. I feel like it's different with *women*. We're supposed to have each other's back. Mothers, daughters, sisters, friends . . ." Leila shakes her head. "Maybe it's just me. I'm not surprised when men let me down, but when women do . . ."

"Like your mother?"

"Yes. She decided that if I wasn't going to be the kind of person she wanted me to be, then her life was easier without me in it. So she let me go, and I understand that. I don't forgive her, but I understand. She didn't miss me at all, just like I didn't miss my girls last weekend, and I don't miss them now." Sensing disapproval, she adds, "But enough about that. I'll shut up now."

After a pause, Molly says, "You know who I don't miss?"

"Ross," Leila and J.J. say in unison.

"Hell, yes!" Molly drawls, and they all laugh. "I don't miss Ross, and I don't miss men. I feel like I spent my whole life depending on them to take care of me. I was that girl who always had to have a boyfriend. Even in college, all I really wanted was to find the right guy and get engaged."

Stef pushes his way into Leila's mind again. Molly had talked of marrying him, back when they were dating.

"But you wanted to be an actress, Molly," J.J. says.

"No, I know, but not like you two, always talking about your careers—Leila was going to start an amazing business . . ."

Leila makes a *pfft* sound. "So much for that."

"And you were going to write the great American novel, J.J."

She makes a face. "What Leila said. At least you did what you wanted to do, Molly. You actually became an actress."

"Community theater didn't pay the bills. I'm not complaining," she adds quickly, as Dawson drains the last of the milk from his bottle. She puts it aside, leans him forward on her lap, and rubs his back. "I'm just saying, I spent all those years searching for the perfect guy—someone I could count on, someone to love, someone who wouldn't leave, someone who'd take care of me because I sure wasn't capable of taking care of myself. And now . . . I've got him! I've got the perfect guy, this little guy, and he's my whole world, the only thing that was missing, the only thing I ever needed. And all I want is to take care of him, and of myself."

"You can, Molly. You can give him everything," Leila tells her.

"You mean, with the lottery money?"

"Isn't that what you mean?"

"Sure, I guess. I mean . . . money is part of it. A huge part. But it's . . ." She pauses at the sound of jingling dog tags and heels tapping across the terrazzo floor in the next room.

Shea Daniels appears. According to her official bio, she's in her early thirties. She appears younger, but carries herself with the poise and command of a seasoned businessperson. She's tan and toned, an understated beauty, effortlessly elegant in a trim black dress, classic pumps, pearls, and a chignon.

Seeing that she's holding a yappy teacup Chihuahua, Leila wonders if she's one of those fancy women who carries a tiny canine as an accessory.

"Welcome to Windfall, ladies . . . oh, and gentleman!"

Dawson responds to that with a loud burp, bringing a round of laughter.

"You must be Dawson," Shea says, pointing in turn, "so you must be Molly . . . J.J. . . . and Leila."

"Impressive," Leila says.

"Well, Justin sent me your info so I did my homework. If you did, too, then you know that I'm Shea. This little fireball is Lola, and Mel—" She turns toward the door. "Mel? Come on, Mel! Shhh, Lola! Sorry, I can get her out of here if you think it'll scare the baby?"

"No, he loves dogs."

Shea sets the little pup on the floor and she races around the room. Sure enough, Dawson breaks into a drooly grin.

"Oh, good. She's harmless. So is Mel."

"That's Mel?" Leila asks, as an Irish wolfhound lumbers into the room.

"Short for Mellow Marshmallow. He's a lovable mush. You'll see. Do you like dogs?"

"Sure," Leila says. "I have cats—I live with my boyfriend and they're his—but I love dogs."

"I grew up with dogs," Molly says, reaching down to pet Mel, who settles on the floor in front of the couch. "He's a sweetheart."

Shea shifts her gaze to Lola, sniffing and barking around J.J.'s ankles. "She'll settle down in a minute or two. Are you okay with her, J.J.? I can put her in another room."

"I'm fine." J.J. gives Lola a cautious pat, then leans back and sips her drink.

Shea pours herself a glass of red wine and joins them, saying that their catered dinner delivery should be arriving soon, along with the rest of her team.

"'There are just so many detours slowing things down tonight. It's—"

"Fire season! That's what I was telling Molly and J.J." Leila can't keep herself from interrupting. "I've lived out here for twenty years now, so I'm used to it, but I remember being rattled when I was new."

She sounds like one of her daughters, trying to impress one of the cool kids, but she can't help it. Shea is the sophisticated self-sufficient entrepreneur Leila wanted to be. And anyway, Shea doesn't seem to mind.

She smiles. "Yes, fire seasons seem to be getting more and more disruptive, don't they? At least you're all here, and settled in. How's everyone holding up?"

"Holding up?" Leila echoes.

"You know . . . the shock of the win, the unexpected travel, dealing with old friends and money . . . it's a lot of stress."

"There are worse things to stress about," Leila points out.

"You're absolutely right, and you have plenty to celebrate this weekend, my friends. Did anyone get a chance to explore the house?"

Leila pauses so that Molly and J.J. can get into the conversation, but they just shake their heads.

"I did," she tells Shea. "Justin said to make myself at home, so . . . I mean, it's such an amazing house."

"Did you do the whole self-guided tour? Check out the view from the top floor?"

"The top floor? No, I wasn't sure I was supposed to go up there, and . . . actually, I was a little spooked," she admits with an embarrassed little laugh.

"Oh?" Shea's gaze is sharp.

"Justin said we were the only ones here, but I could have sworn I heard someone up there. Not that I believe in ghosts."

"Well, I sure do," Molly says. "A lot of old houses have haunted attics."

"This one doesn't even have an attic," Shea points out. "Just a cupola."

"Well, maybe it's a haunted cupola, because I'm pretty sure I saw a ghost flitting around up there when we pulled into the driveway this afternoon. Justin was waiting for me downstairs at the door, and J.J. wasn't here yet, and Leila was outside by the water."

"Right. It's the only place I can get a phone signal."

"It's the wildfires," Shea says. "It happens sometimes, especially when the devil winds kick in."

"Devil winds?" Molly echoes with a shudder.

"That's what we call them around here. Officially, they're the Santa Anas."

"Oh—I've never heard of that, either."

"I have," Leila says.

Before she can go on, J.J. surprises her.

"So have I." J.J. stands, grabs a book from the built-in shelves, and opens it. "Wow. A first edition, huh?"

"What is it?" Molly asks.

"Raymond Chandler. One of my favorites." J.J. turns a page and reads, "'It was one of those hot dry Santa Anas that come down through the mountain passes and curl your hair and make your nerves jump and your skin itch. On nights like that every booze party ends in a fight. Meek little wives feel the edge *of the carving knife and study their husbands' necks. Anything can happen.'"*

She snaps the book closed and returns it to the shelf.

"How the heck did you do that, J.J.?" Leila asks. "Did you plant that creepy book there, or are you magical?"

J.J. laughs. "No, I spotted it earlier. I was checking out the bookshelves while we were talking."

"Of course you were. J.J.'s a writer," Molly tells Shea. "She knows all about literature."

"Speaking of . . ." Leila opens her phone to the photo of the stone marker inscription and passes it to J.J. "Ever heard of this quote?"

"'*He who has gone, so we but cherish his memory, abides with us, more potent, nay, more present than the living man,*'" J.J. reads, and looks up. "No, but I've heard of Antoine de Saint-Exupéry. He wrote *The Little Prince*. It's a classic."

"Did you mention him to me recently, then?" Leila asks.

"No. Why would I?"

"I don't know. Somebody brought him up, but I can't figure out who, or where. When I saw this marker today, the name was so familiar." She turns to Shea. "I'm guessing it's a memorial for Chantal Charbonneau?"

"Yes."

"Do you know anything about it?"

"About the marker?"

"No, the disappearance. Chantal. Were you aware of the history of this house when you bought it?"

"I didn't buy it. I inherited it, from my parents."

"They bought it?"

"They inherited it."

"From . . . ?" Leila prods

"Chantal."

Leila's jaw drops.

"Whoa!" Molly is wide-eyed. "How did that happen?"

"My mother was her housekeeper, and my father took care of the property. Chantal didn't have any family. She treated them very well."

"I guess," Molly says.

"So you . . . did you *know* her?" J.J. asks.

"I was a little girl."

Which doesn't answer the question. But before Leila can ask her to elaborate, Molly speaks up. "There's a painting in my suite, of a woman . . . is it of Chantal? Was that her room when she lived here?"

"The painting was hers. It was there when she lived here, but I don't know that it's *of* her. She collected lots of art. And that wasn't her room."

"Good. I think I'd be afraid she was haunting it."

"Which one was hers?" Leila asks.

"Not the one you're staying in, or yours, either, J.J. I don't use it for guests."

"In case she pops in for a visit?" Leila asks, intrigued.

"I thought you didn't believe in ghosts," Molly says.

"I'm not talking about her ghost. I mean, *her*."

She chuckles. "Well, it's mostly that it's outdated—a true boudoir, right out of the French countryside, with toile wallpaper and poufs and frills everywhere. My parents kept it just as she left it and I guess I've just never felt the need to redecorate."

She changes the subject to tomorrow morning's sessions, covering financial, legal, and security matters.

"I think we all agree that the most pressing matter is laying the groundwork for you to claim your money in the safest, most practical and efficient way," Shea says. "Later in the day, the rest of my team will come in to do presentations on—"

She breaks off at Lola's sudden yapping. Mel stirs and sits up expectantly.

The front door opens and a masculine voice calls, "Hello?"

"Oh." Shea frowns, and she calls, "In the library."

A man appears in the doorway with a Filson duffel bag slung over one broad shoulder. If this were a movie, he'd be playing a cop or government agent—clean-shaven and handsome in a dark suit, with a buttoned-up, authoritative vibe. He's winded, and a strong smell of burnt wood wafts into the room with him.

"Beck. So nice of you to join us," Shea says without a hint of the warmth with which she'd greeted the women. "I was starting to think you weren't going to make it."

"I almost didn't. They've got a barricade a few miles back, so I left the car and came the rest of the way on foot. I would have let you know, but there's no service."

"You don't say."

"Is the landline—"

"No," Shea tells him. "Everything's down."

"What do you mean, there's a barricade?" Molly asks.

"For detours because of the fires," Shea explains.

"No detours now," the man says. "The road is *closed*."

Molly gasps. "You mean we're trapped here?"

The question hangs in the smoky air.

Seeing the grim look that passes between Shea and the newcomer, Leila knows the answer, and her heart begins to pound.

Hi, guys, welcome to *Disappearing Acts.* I'm host Riley Robertson, former investigative reporter, current podcaster, and perennial snoop!

In today's episode of *Whatever Happened to Chantal Charbonneau?* we're going to be playing amateur detective, investigating everything we know about the circumstances of her disappearance.

The wheels seem to have been set in motion four years earlier, when she traveled abroad for the 1997 Cannes Film Festival. In her final public appearance on the red carpet, she told the press that the trip was a homecoming, as she'd spent part of her childhood on the Côte d'Azur.

After the festival, she remained in France for the summer, renting a secluded seaside villa near the Spanish border. She managed to stay out of the spotlight until late August, when she surfaced in Paris and was photographed dining on the Champs-Élysées with an unidentified woman. The next day, just a stone's throw from that spot, Princess Diana was killed after being chased by reporters.

Chantal returned to California and issued a statement that she was pulling out of the film she was about to start shooting, asking for privacy as she took time off to tend to personal business.

Maybe the decision was impromptu, because she was spooked by the paparazzi's role in the princess's death. Or maybe she'd already planned to step back, but timed the announcement so that it would be eclipsed by the loss of a woman whose star outshone her own.

By the time the press caught up with her story that fall, she'd bought Windfall, a secluded seaside villa that bore striking similarities to the one she'd just vacated on the Mediterranean. The tabloids claimed that she'd gone into hiding because she was being stalked by a deranged fan; that she'd had a nervous breakdown; that she was in rehab for addiction. Nobody ever knew the truth.

Chantal never made another film and was never again seen in public. On September 14, 2001—just weeks after the fourth anniversary of Diana's death and days after the September 11 attacks—her housekeeper reported that she'd vanished.

SATURDAY MORNING

MOLLY

A scream jars Molly from a sound sleep.

She gasps, and her lungs fill with smoky air.

Fire! Trapped! Dawson!

She leaps from the bed and races across the dark room.

But it's the wrong direction, the wrong room, a room where there's a plaster wall instead of open space.

She barrels into it full force, slamming her head to blinding pain, and sinks to the floor clutching her skull. It's the kind of pain that makes your stomach roil; the kind that obliterates all coherent thought.

It takes her several seconds to realize that there's tile beneath her, not hardwood, and . . . and . . . and she isn't at home in Savannah, she's in California.

She gets to her feet and feels her way back toward the bed, fumbling for her phone on the nightstand, currently useful only as a clock and a light source. Noting that it's a little past two in the morning, she opens the flashlight app and shines the beam so that it falls on Dawson in the make-shift nursery beyond the archway.

He's sound asleep in his crib, lying on his back as he had been the last time she'd checked him, half-covered by the blanket, one hand clutching his stuffed bear, the other flung over his head.

Her fingertips find a lump just above her forehead. If she was home, she'd get an ice pack for it, but there's no way she's going to prowl around a strange house in the dead of night. Especially this house.

She flicks her gaze to the window. It's open, lace curtains fluttering in a stiff wind that smells of the wildfires still burning out there in the night, cutting them off from the rest of the world.

Shea and Beck had convinced Molly and the others that they're all safe here. Beck had spoken with a utility worker who told him the road is temporarily closed to restrict access for first responders as well as crews working to restore cellular communications.

Shea said it's no accident that this property has survived a century's worth of fire seasons, using unfamiliar phrases like "noncombustible materials" and "defensible space."

Molly wants to believe that this is all very ordinary for Californians in fire season. But a scream in the night is extraordinary in any circumstances . . .

Unless it had come from some animal—a coyote? Are there coyotes here?

Or maybe it was part of a dream. A nightmare.

Maybe it was just the devil wind.

She'd gone back to the library and found the Raymond

Chandler book J.J. had quoted to them, crawling into bed with it and hoping to read herself to sleep.

Big mistake.

She kept rereading the passage about how on nights like this, "*every booze party ends in a fight. Meek little wives feel the edge of the carving knife and study their husbands' necks. Anything can happen.*"

But that's just a story.

Molly closes the windows, turns off the light, and gets back into bed, certain she'll be awake for the remainder of the night, even though she's completely exhausted.

The next time she opens her eyes, the room is bright.

Back home, morning sun floods her room through tall, east-facing windows. Here, the light isn't so much golden as it is murky yellow from the smoky haze that seems to hang over everything, indoors and out.

Someone is knocking on her door.

Molly sits up and winces at the pain in her skull. She gingerly touches the bump, remembering. There was a scream . . .

"Molly?" J.J. calls from the hall. "Are you in there?"

She gets out of bed. Dawson stirs in his crib as she opens the door.

J.J. is there, wearing shorts, sneakers, a T-shirt, and a troubled expression. Her brown hair needs a good brushing, and her face is still pink and now peeling from last weekend's sunburn.

"Molly, is Leila here with you?"

"Leila? What? No! We're sleeping."

"Sorry, but I couldn't call or text you because there's still no signal. I waited as long as I could to knock. I didn't want to wake the baby or upset you, but . . ."

J.J. steps into the room and closes the door behind her.

"Upset me? About what? What happened?"

"Nothing, just . . . I can't find Leila. I thought maybe she was here, or that you'd seen her."

"Maybe she's sleeping."

"It's almost ten."

"Well, we were up so late. What time did we go to bed? Midnight? One?"

"She's Leila, Molly. She never sleeps in."

Hearing Dawson rustling around behind her, Molly turns to see that he's pulled himself to a standing position, clinging to the crib rail with one hand, the other outstretched toward her. She hurries to him, telling J.J., "That was back in college. Maybe she does now."

"She doesn't. In Vegas, she bounced out of bed every morning before six, remember?"

"Maybe she got up at six and now she's taking a nap," Molly says around a yawn. "I just got up and I can use one already."

"Leila doesn't nap. Even after all-nighters, remember? You and I would be out cold the next day and she'd come bounding in, all energetic and wanting us to go do something."

"Again, that was college."

"Well, I knocked on her door loud enough that she would have heard me if she was in there."

Molly lays Dawson on the changing table. Poor baby is damp—sweaty in the stuffy room, and soaked through his diaper.

Leila's voice echoes back from last night. *I've made so many mistakes . . . I'm definitely not a great mom.*

At the time, Molly had found herself judging her friend. Especially when she confessed that she doesn't miss her own children.

But no mom is perfect, she thinks, unsnapping her son's wet onesie. No mom does everything right. She should have said that to Leila.

"Did you look all over the house, J.J.?"

"Yes."

"Even the haunted cupola?"

"It's not haunted, but yes. She's nowhere."

"She can't be nowhere. Everyone is somewhere. She must be outside. She probably went for a swim, or—"

"She's not at the pool, and I looked all over the property."

"Well, she probably left the property. Her daughters are staying with Warren this weekend. Maybe something happened—some kind of family emergency—and Leila had to go down there. Like, one of the girls could have broken an ankle at cheerleading practice or—"

"Cheerleading practice?"

"Or somewhere! Wherever! Or they could have come down with a fever or—"

"Molly. You're forgetting something. Even if that happened, how would Leila have found out?"

"They would have called her and— Oh." Right. There's no phone service. "Or, maybe she called them early this morning to check in and they told her and she left."

"Without telling anyone? And how did she leave? We're miles from anywhere. And the road is closed."

"Okay, then maybe she just . . . went for a walk."

"With fires burning all around us? No. It's way too smoky out there for exercise. Stop grasping at straws, Molly." J.J. paces to the French doors and looks out. "You know what I think? I think she freaked out because we're stranded up here."

"We're all freaked out." Molly pulls one of Dawson's chubby arms out of his onesie. "The wine helped last night, but in the grim light of day . . . I don't like this, and I think we should get out of here."

"I'm guessing that's what Leila did."

Molly turns to stare at J.J. "She wouldn't take off and leave us behind."

"I wouldn't think so, but . . ."

"J.J.! Leila is our friend! She wouldn't just take off without telling us."

"Then where is she, Molly?"

"In her room! I'm sure she's in her room. She was probably just in the shower or something when you checked."

"Okay, I'll go knock again, but—"

"I'll come with you."

Molly quickly finishes changing Dawson, picks him up, and follows J.J. down the hall to Leila's door.

J.J. knocks. "Leila?"

They wait.

Molly knocks, louder. Calls, louder, "Leila!"

They wait again.

Molly reaches out and turns the knob. The door opens.

Stepping over the threshold, she sees Leila's Gucci knockoff purse in the middle of the neatly made bed. And there's the Rollaboard she'd had in Vegas last weekend, sitting on a luggage rack, unzipped and empty. The closet door is open, and several hangers are draped with clothes. Several pairs of shoes are lined up along the bottom.

A cell phone charger is plugged into a wall outlet nearby, with no phone attached to the cord.

"Looks like she's got her phone with her, wherever she is," she tells J.J. "I'll bet she went back out to that spot by the water where she said there's a signal."

"I looked there."

Molly walks to the open window and looks out. "Everything is so smoky, maybe you missed her."

"I guess that's possible. But I was calling for her. She would have heard me."

"Then she must be in the house. Let's go find her."

SHEA

May the dreams you hold dearest be those that come true.

Shea had correctly guessed that sleep would take a while to reclaim her last night, with the wind howling, and the dogs unsettled by the travel, and the air so smoky, and Beck under the same roof.

Mostly that. Yes, there was wind and smoke, and yes, the dogs were more restless than usual, even Mellow Mel. But the problem—at least for Shea—is Beck.

She'd been relieved when he headed upstairs shortly after arriving, saying he was exhausted and would see them all in the morning. She, too, would have preferred retreating behind closed doors to eating sandwiches in the kitchen with three nervous strangers.

"Isn't it dangerous to close off access?" Molly had asked.

"The opposite. That road can be treacherous in this low visibility, especially at night."

"But Beck said they closed it for repairs, so why isn't service restored by now?" Leila asked, having spent the evening continually checking her phone.

"I'm sure they're working on it."

J.J. seemed more anxious than anyone, continually going to the windows to look out into the night. "The smoke is so strong. It smells like everything is on fire right outside the door."

"Because the wind is blowing the smoke this way," Shea said. "The fires are contained, and they're burning a good distance away."

That had been the case when she arrived, anyway. She'd still felt pretty confident last night.

This morning, she isn't so sure. The phones and internet are still down, the air remains thick with smoke, and the hot dry wind is blowing incessantly.

She pulls her hair into a ponytail, skips the makeup, and dresses in jeans, sneakers, and a hoodie. She'll change into business attire when the rest of the team arrives and the meetings can commence, but until they do, she's going for comfort. That's all it is. She isn't just trying to be contradictory to the buttoned-up Beck who'd shown up last night, bearing no resemblance to the laid-back, unshaven, shaggy-haired, madras-clad man she'd last seen nine months ago.

"We don't care what he wears, do we? And we don't care what he thinks about what we wear, either," she tells the dogs, scooping Lola into her arms and beckoning to Mel. "Let's go. Come on."

Stepping into the hall, she glances at the closed door that leads to the cupola, remembering the telescope, wondering who'd been prowling around up there.

The door locks only from the inside with an old-fashioned slide bolt, like every other door in the house. There's no way to restrict access, and there's never been a need.

It couldn't have been Justin. His knees can barely carry him up one flight of stairs; he'd have no reason to ascend three. Anyway, he doesn't smoke, and she'd smelled tobacco.

It might have been someone involved with setting up the nursery or a house cleaner, except . . .

Except that she's been using the same trusted staff for years now, and no one has ever gone to the cupola. She supposes someone might have ventured there to get a view of the wildfires to the east, just as she had. But if that were the case, wouldn't the telescope have been turned in that direction?

Anyway, the staff had vacated the place Thursday night. That spider would have long since repaired its web.

Someone was up there yesterday. It must have been one of the women.

Leila Randolph.

She'd arrived first. She'd shown such an interest in the cliffside promontory where the telescope is aimed, and in the house, and Chantal . . .

It makes sense that she'd have gone snooping around, but why would she have lied about it?

All is still as Shea descends the stairs, with Lola yapping in her arms and Mel lumbering along behind her. On the second floor, all the guestroom doors are closed, including Beck's.

On the main floor, she can smell coffee brewing, mingling only with the scent of smoke and not the fresh-baked cinnamon rolls that should have been delivered by now from a nearby bakery. The road must still be closed.

She opens a door to the courtyard. Lola races out, trailed by Mel. Shea is about to follow them when she hears a pan rattle in the kitchen. Probably J.J. or Molly, making breakfast.

She sticks her head in and sees that it's Beck.

Why can't he be wearing a suit, as he had been yesterday? Why does he have to be in flannel, boots, and jeans, cracking eggs into a bowl like some . . . some morning-after guy.

She's about to slip away when he says, "Hey."

He always did have eyes in the back of his head.

"Hey." She returns the greeting and steps into the kitchen. This is, after all, *her* house.

She pours dog food into two metal bowls and opens a door leading into the courtyard. "Here, Lola! Mel!"

They ignore her, romping in the fountain. She puts the bowls on the ground and reluctantly steps back into the kitchen, leaving the door ajar.

"There's coffee," Beck says, whisking the eggs.

"I see that."

"No pastries, so I'm making an omelet."

"I see that, too." She grabs a mug from the cabinet then goes to the coffeepot.

Behind her, the refrigerator opens and closes. A moment later, as she pours the steaming brew into her cup, a container of cream slides across the counter toward her.

Cream. Not half and half, not creamer, not skim milk

or whole milk or almond milk or whatever other milks are stocked in the fridge.

He's close enough that his familiar scent envelops her. It isn't cologne; he's your basic bar of soap and drugstore shampoo kind of man. But he always smells of cedar and soap and spearmint, and . . .

And how she takes her coffee is far from the most intimate detail he knows about her.

"Thanks," she murmurs. "And thanks for taking the assignment."

"Yeah, well, Justin asked, and I was available, so . . ."

"So." She pours cream into her cup. "I had no idea he'd called you, or that you were even back in LA."

"Ah. Then I'm not here at your special request."

"What? No! I—"

She turns and sees that his mouth is bent into . . .

Not a smile, exactly. More a smirk.

She turns away and stirs her coffee for far longer than is necessary. "I was expecting Abi."

"There was a death in his family."

"I know. His sister."

"It's tragic. Are you . . . ?"

"Am I what?" She turns to look at him.

"Okay," he says. "Are you okay."

"I'm sad for Abi. I didn't know her."

He nods.

She's relieved to hear footsteps in the next room, and voices calling, "Leila? Leila!"

"She must be around here someplace." Shea recognizes the Southern drawl. Molly.

"Then why isn't she answering us?" The other voice belongs to J.J., the softspoken one.

A moment later she strides into the kitchen, dressed in jeans and sneakers. Molly is behind her in a ruffled nightgown, balancing her son on her hip.

"Ladies? Is everything all right?" Shea asks.

"We can't find Leila. We just checked the whole house, and J.J. looked outside. Her— Ouch!" Molly winces as her son pulls at her blond bangs. She leans into the tug and attempts to extract his grasping fingers.

"Molly, did you hit your head?" Shea asks, spotting a bruised lump on her forehead.

"Oh—yes. I walked into a wall in the middle of the night and nearly knocked myself right out."

Beck peers at her. "That looks pretty painful. Are you sure you don't have a concussion?"

"Right now, I'm not worried about me. I'm worried about Leila. I heard a scream. That's why I got up in the dark at that hour."

"Which hour?" he asks.

"Just past two."

"She said the scream came from outside," J.J. adds. "She had her windows open. I didn't because of the smoke. I didn't hear a thing."

"I didn't, either. And my windows were closed," Beck says, and looks at Shea.

"Same."

"Well, all y'all don't live in the Deep South. I'm used to air-conditioning. The room felt so hot and stuffy that I thought I'd get fresh air. I'd had some wine, so I guess I wasn't thinking things through—I didn't realize it was hotter outside, and so smoky. Anyway, when I heard that scream, I closed the window."

"And you weren't concerned?" Beck asks. "You didn't think you should check it out?"

"Of course, I was concerned! I mean, a woman screaming in the night . . . that's a terrifying thing to wake up to. But I had the baby there, sleeping, and then I hit my head, and then I thought . . . I don't know. I thought it was just a coyote."

Shea isn't surprised that Molly sounds defensive. She wants to remind Beck that he's here as a security consultant, not law enforcement. Right now, they need to keep everyone calm and figure out what's going on.

If Shea was right about Leila Randolph poking around the cupola yesterday, she's very likely on the premises, looking for Chantal's ghost or clues or whatever.

"It probably was a coyote, or a bobcat," Shea tells Molly, avoiding Beck's gaze. "Bobcats sound exactly like a woman screaming. And the fires destroy wildlife habitats and displace animals, so they're on the move right now."

"That makes sense," J.J. says.

"It does, but now that Leila's gone . . ."

"I'm sure she's around here somewhere," Shea tells Molly.

"That's what I thought. Like maybe she went for a

walk—you know, on the beach or something. But J.J. says there's no beach."

"There isn't," Beck tells her. "The whole property is a cliff. There are no steps, no way down to the water, and nothing but boulders and cliffs there."

"And everything is so smoky," J.J. adds. "It would be treacherous to go walking around out there."

Dawson whimpers. Molly shushes him and bounces him on her hip. "Sorry, he's hungry."

Beck walks to the door that leads out to a wide back terrace, shaded by the overhead balcony. Cupping a hand above his eyes, he presses his head close to the glass, scanning the area. Then he turns back to the women.

"Are you sure she's not just asleep in her room?" he asks.

J.J. shakes her head. "She's not. We looked. The door's unlocked and all her stuff is there—her clothes, her purse."

"Not her phone," Molly says. "I bet she went out by the water to call home or check her texts. Or maybe she's just exploring the house."

"But why didn't she hear us calling her?" J.J. asks.

"Maybe she tripped and fell, like I did. Maybe that's the scream I heard. Maybe she knocked herself out or something."

Something . . .

Shea notes the glint in Beck's eye as he turns away from the window and is certain his thoughts parallel her own.

When the woman in possession of a shared billion-dollar, bearer-specific lottery ticket disappears, you'd better hope the reason is as innocuous as a bump on the head.

J.J.

Noting the glance that passes between Shea and Beck, J.J. feels her legs go liquid.

They don't think Leila tripped and fell. They think . . .

What the hell do they think?

Her heart pounds. She turns to Molly, who meets her gaze, wide-eyed.

"I think it's a good idea to search again," Beck says, mostly to Shea. "Inside and out."

"I agree. I'll check the house while you check outside."

"I think we'd better stick together."

"It would be a lot faster if we split up."

"It would be a lot safer if we stick together."

"Safer, how?" Molly asks him. "You don't think there's anything dangerous going on, do you?"

"I don't know what to think. Until we know more, I think you two might want to head to your rooms. Or at least, stay right here," he adds, catching Shea's scowl.

"I have to go upstairs and feed Dawson," Molly says.

"I'll come with you."

J.J. follows her up to her room. Molly closes the door after them, slides the bolt, and turns to her.

"J.J., I really think Leila is just off exploring. She said she was going to play Nancy Drew and find out what happened to Chantal."

"Yes, but I thought she meant all three of us. We would be her Bess and George." At Molly's blank look, she explains, "Nancy's best friends."

"Is there any book you don't know everything about? I couldn't believe it last night when you whipped out that story about the Santa Ana winds. By the way, it gave me nightmares, so thanks a lot. Can you please hold Dawson while I get his breakfast?"

"He doesn't know me. Won't he freak out?"

"Just for a minute. It's so hard to do everything one-handed."

J.J. takes the baby and shifts her position awkwardly. Dawson offers her a slimy, toothless grin and it comes right back to her—how to hold a wriggly baby, straddling him over her right hip and giving his shoulder a reassuring pat. Enveloped in his milk and powder scent, she remembers her own son at this age.

Brian wasn't fair-haired, blue-eyed, or chubby like Dawson. He was lean and spindly even in infancy, with sparse brown fuzz on his head and an intensely curious dark gaze. He didn't babble and burble as Dawson does, either. He was quiet and introspective from the start. She and John used to joke that he was a grown man trapped in a baby's body.

"I bet when he starts talking, he's never going to shut up," J.J. used to say, and John agreed.

They were wrong. Brian turned out to be a man of few words. Too few words, as far as she's concerned.

"But then, we're not exactly chatterboxes ourselves," John said once when she complained that she had no idea what was going on in their teenage son's life. "And boys that age don't share with their parents."

"Do they share with anyone?"

"I know I didn't."

"Sometimes you still don't, even with me," she said, and John couldn't argue with that. He'd had a difficult childhood he never liked to discuss, and he spared her most details of his job so that she wouldn't worry.

Dawson fusses, squirming in her arms as Molly removes the tray from the high chair. "Mama's coming, sweetie. Hang on, hang on."

The baby's fist closes around J.J.'s glasses.

"No!" she says sharply, as he twists the frames off her head.

Startled by her outburst, he lets out a wail. Molly whirls, reaching for her son.

"What happened?"

"He . . . just . . . my glasses." J.J. hands over the baby and examines the frames. One side is badly mangled, crooked where it meets the hinge.

"He didn't mean it," Molly tells her, as Dawson cries in her arms.

"I know he didn't mean it. Of course he didn't mean it, but . . ."

"I'm sure they can be fixed. Just twist them back."

She tugs at them and tries them on. They slide down her nose at a slant.

"Oh, no. Did you bring another pair?"

"I don't even *have* another pair. Our insurance only covers one a year. And I'm pretty much blind without my glasses." She pulls off the glasses and again attempts to bend them into shape, hands trembling.

She hears John's voice in her head, talking to her over the crying baby. The baby is Brian, and J.J. is in bed, staring at the ceiling, not caring.

What's wrong with you, babe? John is asking. *Why are you like this?*

Oh, John. Oh, Brian. I'm so sorry . . .

"I'm so sorry."

The voice is Molly's, in real life, dragging her back to the present.

"I just can't believe he broke your glasses. I feel awful about this."

"Oh . . . please don't. It's okay. I'll just get a new pair."

"But I'll pay for it. I can— Wait! Who even cares about what insurance covers?" At J.J.'s blank stare, Molly says, "We're rich, remember?"

"Oh. Yes. Just . . ."

"Just what?"

"Not until we turn in that ticket. Until then, everything is the same."

"I know, but we're going to turn it in. It's not like that's changed."

They stare at each other for a long moment.

"J.J.? You know that, right? Everything's going to be okay."

Molly is the kind of person who needs to believe that.

And J.J. is the kind of person who needs to let her.

She forces a smile. "Of course, Molly. Everything's going to be great."

SHEA

"Okay, if you're going to work for me, you can't send two grown women to their rooms like they're children," Shea tells Beck, as soon as they step out onto the terrace.

"I didn't mean it to sound that way. I'm just trying to contain the situation. You know that I—"

"This isn't a crime scene. These are my clients."

"And one of them is missing."

"Not missing. Just unaccounted for."

The dogs bound over and Beck bends to pet them. "Hey, Lola. Hey, Mel. Remember me?"

They lick his hand. Traitors.

Shea heads toward the gate. "The smoke is getting pretty thick, Beck. Last night, when you said they closed the road just to make repairs, you were being honest, right?"

"That's what the workman told me."

She shrugs. "Okay."

"I wouldn't lie, Shea."

"Okay."

"But this isn't a great situation. We should think about evacuating."

"No," she says, though she'd just been thinking the same thing. But when he says black, she can't seem to keep herself from saying white.

"No?"

"If there's a mandatory evacuation, they'll let us know."

"How? It's not like we can get a call, or text."

"They go from house to house, and they drive around with bullhorns making announcements. Believe me, this isn't the worst the smoke has ever been here. The house is protected, and it's been around for decades."

Beck catches up with her at the gate, along with Mel and Lola.

"Hey, you two can't come with us," she says, bending to pat their heads, and wishing she hadn't made that word choice.

Us.

She slides the bolt and pushes the gate, positioning herself in the opening so that the dogs can't slip through.

"Coming?" she asks Beck. "You can wait here if you—"

"I'm coming."

The gate leads from the courtyard past a pool area and tennis courts. No Leila. They call her name, but there's no reply.

The pool house is empty, as are the nearby garden and toolsheds. All are dusty and undisturbed. Shea makes note of the cobwebs and spiderwebs, again thinking of the cupola. She opts not to tell Beck about it, though she isn't sure why. If this were six months ago, or a year ago . . .

But things are different now.

"There's a lot more ground to cover. Maybe we should go back and check the house before we search the rest of the property," she suggests.

"Her friends said they looked everywhere. You don't believe them?"

"No, I do. Don't you?"

He shrugs.

"You don't?"

"Until she turns up, I'm not trusting anything anyone says. You know as well as I do that when there's a billion dollars in the mix, people do crazy things."

A billion dollars . . . and the devil winds.

She points toward the water. "Since she's got her phone, she might be out there, looking for cell service. Let's go."

Calling Leila's name, they follow the winding path toward the sea, and then along the cliff that spans the property's western border. It's steep in some areas and rutted in others, bordered by a clearing on one side, the sea on the other. Smoke swirls like fog in Jack the Ripper's London, but every so often, the wind shifts, allowing a hint of September sunlight.

"Leila!" Shea calls, scanning the hazy landscape as the promontory comes into view.

No Leila sitting there in one of the blue Adirondack chairs checking her texts, or snapping photos of the stone marker.

"You know, the thing that makes this property so damned private is the one thing that could help right now," he comments.

"Electronic surveillance?"

"Yes."

"This was Chantal's house. She never wanted any of that."

"But it's your house now."

"Yeah, well, I don't want any of that, either."

"Why not?"

"I have my reasons."

"But—"

"We've been over this before," she reminds him, and wishes she hadn't. She doesn't want to acknowledge, to herself and certainly not to him, that they have a past in which he was entitled to offer opinions on her private life, and she occasionally heeded his advice.

Not about the surveillance, though. Never about that, for reasons she wouldn't have shared with him even back then.

She pulls her phone out of her pocket. There's a signal. Weak, but there. She sees several missed calls and a number of texts—Justin, Morgan, Elizabeth, other members of her team, and numbers she doesn't recognize. They can wait, all of them, for at least a few more minutes.

"I'm going to try calling her," she tells Beck.

"You think she's going to answer?"

She shrugs, finding an email with Leila's contact information and dialing her number. It rings directly into voice mail. She hangs up without leaving a message and sends a text instead.

It's Shea. Are you okay?

She sends it, then mounts the platform and surveys the stretch of coast below. The tide is going out, leaving boulders jutting above the waterline.

Beck comes to stand beside her.

"I hate to say it, but she might have been here and wandered too close to the edge and . . ."

"But there's a railing, and a lot of ground before the drop-off. And there are signs posted everywhere. It would be hard to take an accidental fall."

"Right. Maybe she jumped, like Chantal."

She gives him a sharp look.

"What? It wasn't suicide? So, murder?"

"You know I don't talk about that."

"I do know."

He's one of the few people in this world—perhaps the only one—who's ever respected that.

"What I don't know," he goes on, "is whether *you* know."

"That I don't talk about it? I'm aware."

He gives her a look. "That's not what I meant. I'm just wondering whether the truth about Chantal died with her, or whether she's even dead. I mean, she could be an old lady living in France under another identity."

"Is that what you believe?" She keeps her gaze on the scrubby undergrowth between the railing and the drop-off.

"I believe that some people have no problem checking out of their lives, one way or another."

"And you think that's what happened?"

"With Chantal?"

"Or with Leila Randolph." She checks her phone. There's an error message beside the text she'd tried to send, and the cellular bars have disappeared altogether. "My phone's not working. Is yours?"

Beck checks. "No service."

"This is crazy." She pockets the phone.

"You think Leila just checked out? Is that it?"

"I know nothing about her life. I suppose anything is possible."

"But suicide?" Beck asks. "Most people would say a woman in her shoes had everything to live for."

"Most people would have said that about Chantal. I think—I know, better than anyone—that a fortune can destroy a person. I'm not talking about Chantal."

"Leila hadn't even claimed the money yet," Beck points out. "What are the odds that winning made her dive off a cliff right after she got here?"

"Probably a hell of a lot slimmer than the odds of winning the money in the first place."

"Exactly."

"But that's not the only way out, Beck."

"You think she ran."

She hesitates, then nods. "I do. I think she ran."

MOLLY

Twisting the top off a jar of organic banana puree, Molly says, "Wow, fancy. This stuff costs three times as much as the brand I give him back home."

"Shea bought it for you?" J.J. asks.

"It was all here waiting." She gestures around the nursery. "The food, the high chair, the toys, everything. These people cater to your every whim. I wouldn't be surprised if they even made sure your favorite books were downstairs in the library."

"Well, they wouldn't know my favorite books. And I like all books."

"Still . . . I feel like Shea made such an effort to make us feel at home."

"Mmm."

Molly spoons more food into Dawson's open mouth and glances over at J.J.

She's by the fireplace, peering up at the painting above the mantel. Her eyes are anxious and seem oddly small and close-set without the glasses. Her face is covered in scaly white patches, the remnants of the peeling sunburn she'd gotten in Vegas.

"That's the one," Molly comments.

"What's the what?"

"That's the painting I was asking about last night, remember? I asked Shea whether that woman is Chantal, or whether the painting belonged to her."

"You did?"

"You were there."

"Yeah, well, so was gin. Too much gin, thanks to our friend Leila."

Leila—where are you?

What if—

No. Molly won't allow her mind to go to that terrifying place.

"So what did Shea say?" J.J. asks, pointing at the painting. "*Is* that Chantal?"

"She doesn't know. But she mentioned that Chantal's room here is untouched since the day she disappeared. Maybe that's where Leila is."

"We already searched the whole house for her."

"But we just knocked on doors and called her name and stuck our heads in. We didn't go into the rooms. We didn't check bathrooms and closets. Maybe she accidentally got trapped in one."

"Why would she be in a *closet?*"

"Because old houses have doors that stick, and—" Dawson jerks around in his chair, wanting more food. She quickly dips the spoon into the jar. "And they have secret passageways, and hidden rooms."

"And that's where you think Leila is?"

"J.J., I swear I'm not making this up. I grew up in an old house and I live in one now."

"I'm not arguing with you."

"But I feel like you think I'm crazy. Think about it. About Leila. She's so into this Chantal mystery. Did you listen to that podcast she told us about?"

"Not yet. I downloaded it before I left home, though."

"So did I. Anyway . . . I think we should go find Chantal's room."

"*Now?*"

"Yes. I feel like that's where Leila is."

"Do you know which room it is?"

"I'm sure it won't be hard to figure out." She spoons the last of the banana into Dawson's mouth. "I'm just going to throw on some clothes. Watch him for a second."

She rummages through her suitcase. Everything in it strikes her as dowdy, now that she's met Shea Daniels and seen her dressed up and dressed down.

She really needs to get some new clothes. Before Dawson came along, she'd taken such pride in her appearance.

That pretty face of yours is going to open a lot of doors for you, her high school drama coach had promised her, when she told him she planned to study acting in college. *But you'd better have the talent to back it up.*

Apparently, she does not. And the pretty face that opened doors for a couple of decades now looks world-weary with a network of fine wrinkles around the mouth and eyes that her mother calls laugh lines.

Only, Molly hasn't done much laughing lately.

She finds shorts and a T-shirt and dashes into the bathroom.

Two minutes later, she's back—not entirely presentable, but at least no longer in pajamas, and her teeth are brushed, if not her hair.

J.J. has cleaned Dawson's sticky hands with a wipe and removed the plastic tray, fumbling with the harness fastened across his midsection as he squirms.

Molly shoves her feet into flip-flops and lifts Dawson from the chair. He protests loudly and pulls her hair. "Ouch! That hurts Mommy's bump!"

"How's your head feeling?" J.J. asks.

"It just aches," she admits, shifting the baby to her other hip. "But I'm sure part of that's from the wine, and the stress."

"I don't know." J.J. brushes Molly's hair back with a gentle hand and squints at her head. "You might have a concussion."

"Well, I'll ask Dr. Leila what she thinks when we find her. That'll make her day."

J.J. smiles. "Come on. Let's go check her room, just in case."

They hurry down the hall to her door. Molly doesn't bother to knock, turning the knob and disappointed when it opens. "Hey, Leila? Are you here?"

Her voice seems to echo in the quiet house. Somewhere downstairs, a dog barks.

Molly closes the door and surveys the long hallway. Other than her suite, Leila's, and J.J.'s, there are two more rooms at the front of the house. She's certain one of them must have belonged to Chantal.

She's wrong. Beck is staying in the first room, his Filson bag sitting on the luggage rack. The other is empty, but it isn't a boudoir by any stretch of the imagination.

"I guess it's down one of those halls, at the back of the house. It seems strange."

"Well, she did like her privacy," J.J. says. "Do you want to check that wing and I'll do this one?"

"Sure. Holler if you find anything."

Molly heads down the nearest corridor. There are four closed doors. The first is for a bedroom. It's good-sized and furnished in modern neutrals, but it's not suitable for the lady of the house, with no adjoining bath, no balcony, no fireplace—and of course, no wallpaper, and no Leila. The next door along the hall is for a shared bathroom. The third room is nearly identical to the first.

"One left," she tells Dawson growing fussy on her hip. She turns the knob, calling, "Leila?"

This is a corner room, larger than the others, with a fireplace, private bath, and dressing room. Tall windows face the back of the property and you might be able to see the ocean from here on a clear day. French doors open onto the balcony that surrounds the courtyard on three sides.

If this were Molly's house, she might choose this room for herself. It's more private than the others, tucked away back here, and the outdoor stairway down to the courtyard is just outside the door.

Glancing across at the French doors on the parallel stretch of balcony, Molly wonders if that corner room is similar to this one. If so, it must have belonged to Chantal.

As she walks away from the window, she hears a sudden barking in the courtyard below. Turning, she's just in time to see a figure dart from the room opposite toward the balcony staircase.

Hurrying to the French doors, she fumbles, one-handed, with the lock. By the time she gets it open and steps out onto the balcony, calling for Leila, there's nothing to see. No one on the stairs or in the courtyard.

Shea's two dogs are there, though. The Chihuahua is barking wildly at the wrought-iron fence, and even the Irish wolfhound is on his feet, gazing in that direction. Molly sees that the bougainvillea vines are stirring—disturbed by the wind, or by a person who just escaped through the gate.

J.J.

"J.J.?"

Molly's voice floats to her from the other side of the house.

"Coming!" She hurries down the long main corridor. Molly emerges at the other end with Dawson on her hip, his head on her shoulder.

"Did you find Chantal's room?" J.J. calls.

"No, but I just saw . . . someone."

"You saw *someone?*"

"*Something.* I think . . . I don't know. I was down there." She gestures at the short corridor behind her.

"What happened?"

"I had checked all the rooms, and then in the last one, I looked out the window, and . . ." She takes a deep breath. "I thought I saw someone come out of the opposite room on the opposite balcony and hurry down the steps, but . . ." She shakes her head rapidly, wincing as she does so.

"Your head, Molly. Is it hurting?"

"Yes, but . . . are you listening to me, J.J.? I saw someone."

"You said you *thought* you saw someone."

"I *saw* someone."

"Not Leila?"

"It might have been. It was so quick, and I saw it out of the corner of my eye. I went out and called her name, though. Whoever it was would have been in earshot. Leila wouldn't have run away from *me*."

"Then was it Shea? Or Beck?"

"I don't know. All I saw was a blur of a figure, slipping outside and running down the steps. And the dogs were barking."

"I heard them. And, Molly . . . I checked three of the rooms in the other hallway, but the one at the end was locked. I knocked, and I was calling for Leila."

"If she was in there, she would have answered you. It must have been someone else. Or just a ghost."

"I don't believe in ghosts."

"I know you don't. And you know I do. But . . . J.J., what if something happened to the ticket?"

J.J. stares at her. "What do you mean? What could happen?"

"I don't even want to think about it."

"Well, it's in the bank, right?"

"That's what Leila said."

"I even asked her about it yesterday, because . . ."

When she trails off, Molly asks, "Why *were* you asking her, J.J.?"

"I had a run-in with someone at my bank just the other day, and it just . . . it made me wonder."

"About whether you trust Leila?"

"No! About whether I trust the bank!"

"Well, I don't know if that's what Leila got from that. Maybe that's why she reacted that way."

"Reacted how?"

"She seemed defensive. Or maybe *cagey* is a better word."

J.J. stares at her.

"You don't think so?"

"No. I mean, yes. I guess I didn't really want to think about it, but yes. She did seem a little cagey. But we know Leila."

Or do we?

"Right. She doesn't like anyone to question her judgment. Anyway . . . come on. I'll show you where I saw . . . whatever I saw."

As Molly leads her back down the short hallway, J.J. confirms that this wing is laid out exactly as the one she'd explored. Two smaller rooms with a bathroom between them.

Molly opens the last door and they step into a large room.

J.J. goes directly to the window facing the opposite wing and looks out. "That's where you thought you saw someone?"

"That's where I saw someone, yes."

J.J. supposes it's possible.

She unlocks the French door, steps out into the smoky air, and crosses to the railing. In the courtyard below, the dogs spot them and begin to bark.

"Wait, where are you going?" Molly asks as J.J. heads

toward the wrought-iron staircase leading down to the courtyard.

"To look around. Come on, I need you. I can't see anything without my glasses."

Molly hurries after her. At the foot of the stairs, Lola yaps around their feet, and Mel lumbers over to greet them.

Dawson makes a happy gurgling sound, delighted by the dogs.

"I wish y'all could talk," Molly says. "I know you saw someone, too, didn't you?"

J.J. looks around the courtyard. The second-floor balcony sits above a series of arches and pillars, with a covered walkway along the first-floor perimeter.

Molly gasps. "J.J.! Does it look like the French door is open up there?"

She squints at it. "Everything's so blurry to me, I can't tell. Let's go look."

They hurry across the courtyard to the stairway and up to the balcony. The French door to the locked room is, indeed, slightly ajar.

"I *knew* I saw someone," Molly breathes, pushing the door open a little wider and looking inside.

"Well if it wasn't Leila, and Shea and Beck are off somewhere, and we're the only ones here . . . then who?"

"Chantal's ghost," Molly says. "Or Chantal herself. This is definitely her room."

J.J. follows her into what can only be described as a boudoir—toile wallpaper, poufs, frills, and all. It's very different from the other guest rooms. Not just because there's floral bedding and ruffled curtains, but this one appears lived in. There are clothes in the closet, shoes on the shoe rack, and toiletries lined up on a skirted dressing table with an old-fashioned mirror bordered by Edison bulbs. A crystal ashtray sits on the bedside table with a Louis Vuitton cigarette case and gold-plated lighter beside it.

"Oh—see that pink jacket? It's Chanel. I know it is." Molly checks the tag and gasps. "I was right. These have to be Chantal's."

J.J. leaves her sliding hangers along the bar and looks over the rest of the room. There's nothing very personal. No framed photographs, or mail addressed to Chantal, or a diary . . . nothing like that. But it's easy to imagine a fading movie star in this room.

The door is indeed locked from the inside. J.J. slides the bolt and looks out into the deserted hall.

"This has to be her room, don't you think?" Molly asks. "It's just like Shea said. Just like Chantal left it."

"*If* she left it."

"You think that person I saw, sneaking out of the room—maybe it really was Chantal?"

"I think it's—" J.J. breaks off at urgent barking in the courtyard and hurries back out to the balcony just in time to see Shea and Beck step through the gate.

She instinctively steps back, as though she's about to get caught doing something she shouldn't be doing.

Too late. Beck looks up and spots her. He nudges Shea and she, too, glances up.

"Looks like you've found Chantal's room."

"We were just . . . Molly and I are just . . ."

Molly joins her on the balcony, stepping close to J.J. and shifting Dawson's weight to the other side, using him to conceal her face as she says under her breath, "Don't tell them I saw someone, okay? I'll explain, just . . . shhh."

"Can you both come down here, please?" Beck calls. "We have something to discuss."

J.J. breaks into a cold sweat as they slowly descend the staircase. Even from this distance, without her glasses, she can tell that something's terribly wrong.

SHEA

It was Shea's idea to escort the women inside for this difficult conversation. Beck would have broken the news to them right out there in the courtyard, with Molly wrestling a wriggly baby from one hip to the other and J.J. looking as though she's bracing herself for something unpleasant.

They make a detour to the kitchen for coffee.

Beck's abandoned omelet reminds Shea that an hour earlier, his presence in this house was her biggest concern. Now she's not only resigned to it, but relieved to have him here. For the most part.

Until Dawson's flailing hand knocks a mug off the counter and it shatters on the floor and Beck says under his breath to Shea, "Your worst nightmare."

"A broken mug? I don't think so."

"I mean, kids. You hate kids."

"I don't hate them," she protests, glad the others can't hear him over the baby's startled wails and Molly's profuse apologizing.

She doesn't typically give them much thought one way

or another. There are none in her life, and she's never been any more interested in having a family than she's been in marriage.

Well, *never* isn't entirely accurate. Years ago, decades ago, she supposes she'd imagined that she might grow up to become a wife and mother one day. But that was before she lost every person who'd ever mattered to her. Every place she'd ever called home. Every dream she'd held dearest.

"Beck, would you mind grabbing a broom and dustpan from the mudroom and cleaning up the mess while we get settled in the other room?" she asks sweetly.

"No, I'll get it," Molly says quickly, "if you don't mind holding the baby while I—"

"Beck's got it," Shea tells her, and leads the way to the library.

They settle into the library, both women gravitating to the same seats they'd had last night.

Molly settles on the couch, leaving her mug on the table after a few sips and clutching her son on her lap as if someone might snatch him from her arms. Yesterday's makeup is smudged beneath her eyes.

J.J. perches in a chair by the bookshelf. She's no longer wearing her glasses, making the deep trenches beneath her eyes more prominent. Her hands are wrapped around her coffee mug as if seeking warmth on a winter day, when in reality the room is stuffy, windows closed against the smoke. She strikes Shea as a straight shooter, compared to Molly's Pollyanna.

Even Shea chooses the same chair.

Beck joins them, positioning himself in the doorway as if to protect them—or keep them from escaping.

"What's going on?" J.J. asks. "I mean, you didn't find her, and neither did we, so . . ."

"We found this." Shea holds up the sapphire pendant on a delicate gold chain. The clasp is broken, as if someone yanked it from Leila's neck.

J.J. gasps, and Molly lets out a little cry.

Beck states the obvious. "You recognize it."

"Where did you find it?" Molly asks.

"Outside." Shea pauses, wondering how much to tell them and how to phrase it.

"*Where* outside?"

"By the water. I thought Leila might have been wearing it last night," she adds, though she doesn't *think* it, she *knows*.

"Yes, with her blue dress," Molly says.

Shea turns it over and holds it up. "But the initials engraved on the back aren't hers."

"Initials?"

"S.G."

"For September Girls," J.J. explains.

"Yes, that's what we've always called ourselves, because we met in September and our birthdays are . . ." Molly's voice breaks and she looks down.

"Our birthdays are in September, too," J.J. fills in. "September Girls. It's our thing. The three of us."

Shea swallows an unexpected lump in her throat.

"We all have one," Molly goes on. "We were all going to wear them all weekend, but I couldn't get my act together."

J.J. smiles a sad smile. "I couldn't, either. Leila was the organized one. Always."

"So you *all* have one of these necklaces?" Beck asks, rubbing his razor stubble. "They're identical?"

"Right. Mine's upstairs. I haven't even had a chance to unpack my bag yet. You brought yours, too, right, J.J.?"

"Yes. It's in my room."

Shea glances at Beck. He raises an eyebrow at her. She knows what he's thinking.

Don't, she thinks. *Not yet. Just let them digest this for a minute.*

Too late.

"Would you mind making sure?" he asks.

J.J. frowns. "Making sure . . . that my necklace is in my room?"

"Please. You, too, Molly. Just so we can be certain that this one is Leila's."

"That doesn't make sense. We didn't wear ours. Leila did. So that must be hers. She must have dropped it while she was out there checking her messages. I saw her coming back with her phone right before we all met in the library."

"She had it on in the library," Shea says. "She might have gone back out there, though, after the rest of us went to bed."

"She might have," Beck agrees. "But if you ladies

wouldn't mind checking to make sure your necklaces are accounted for . . ."

"You mean, right now? Do you really want me to lug the baby all the way back upstairs again?" Molly asks. "He's so heavy."

"I can check for you, if you tell me where to look," he offers. "Or Shea can hold the baby for you."

"Or you can," Shea shoots back.

"That's all right, I've got him," Molly says, getting to her feet. "J.J., you coming?"

"Right behind you."

MOLLY

"Shh. Come into my room," Molly whispers to J.J. at the top of the steps, as she starts to turn in the opposite direction toward her own suite. "I need to tell you something."

J.J. nods and follows her to her room.

Molly sets Dawson in his bouncy seat and hands him a board book while J.J. quickly locks the door and turns to her with a questioning look.

"He's got a gun, J.J."

"Who does? Beck?"

"Yes, Beck! Who else? Dawson?"

"Okay, well . . . how do you know?"

"I can tell." She'd seen his hand brush against his side in a brief, barely perceptible gesture, but one she recognizes. She'd seen her daddy make the same motion, and Ross, too, over the years. It's what you do when you're carrying a weapon, and you think you might need it.

J.J. says nothing, mouth tight.

"You have to believe me."

"I do believe you, Molly. This is just so crazy."

"I know. And I'm starting to get really freaked out about Leila being gone, you know? Like any minute now, she's going to show up."

She's been picturing it—how they'll all have a good laugh over good champagne.

"Come on, you guys . . . did you really think I'd take off with that ticket?" Leila will ask, and Molly and J.J. will lie that of course they hadn't thought that, not even for a split second.

"We just thought you'd been abducted," Molly will add, and then J.J. will joke that the kidnappers would have brought Leila back in a hurry because she'd drive them crazy.

J.J. nods. "I keep thinking the same thing. That there's some logical explanation, but now . . ."

"I know. Now they've got her necklace, and they're telling us they found it out by the water."

"You don't think that's what happened?"

"Well, this whole thing with Windfall—they tell us not to trust anyone, even our own families, but why would we trust them?"

"That's why you don't want them to know you saw someone sneaking around?"

"The less we tell them about anything, the better. What if this whole thing is a trap? What if they lured us here so they could steal the ticket?"

"They couldn't, if Leila put it into the bank."

"What if she didn't?" Molly asks. "Maybe that's why she was so cagey about it when you asked her. Maybe Shea convinced her to bring it here instead."

"And Leila lied to us about it?"

"Well, not lied, exactly. Just . . . not told us."

"That's the same thing."

"Not really. She'd have known we wouldn't have thought that was a good idea. And once she gets her mind set on something, you know how she is. She was so bent on hiring them, she didn't want to hear any opposition from us."

J.J. nods slowly. "It's not out of the realm of possibility. Not with Leila. So if those two did something to her—"

"Or maybe not them. Maybe someone else."

"Someone else who knew about the ticket."

"Gib?" Molly asks. "She said he's the only one she told."

"Unless she lied about that, too."

"J.J., come on. She's our friend, not someone who . . . lies."

"Molly, you of all people know that anyone can pretend to be someone else."

It's true, and not just because of her theatrical training, though J.J. doesn't know the whole story.

There had been a time when Molly would have told her everything. As roommates for four years, the September Girls had shared so many secrets.

Molly thinks of the one she'd been tempted to confide in Leila and J.J. last weekend. It wouldn't have been the most intimate thing she'd ever confessed to her friends, but in the old days, she could have anticipated exactly how each of them would react. Now, though, she held back.

She's pretty sure she's not the only one keeping aspects of her current life to herself. J.J. has never been one to volunteer personal information. Even know-it-all, tell-it-all Leila had sidestepped certain questions.

"I know people aren't always who they seem to be, J.J. But Leila would never . . . do what you're thinking."

"You're thinking it, too."

She's right. Molly is thinking about it, but she's been trying not to, from the moment Leila wasn't where she was supposed to be.

"You heard what she said last night. How she was mocking her daughters."

"She was joking around. You know that. You even told her to stop making you laugh because it made your sunburn hurt."

"But she does that. She always has. She says something wildly inappropriate and then turns it into this funny act to distract us from focusing on whatever she said."

"What was so wildly inappropriate?"

"It's just . . . look, I'd never in a million years mock John or Brian, or say that I wouldn't miss them." Suddenly, J.J. looks as though she might cry. "Or that . . . or that I didn't care if I never saw them again. And you wouldn't say that about Dawson, either."

Molly looks down at her son. "That's different. John's your husband, Brian's deployed. Dawson's just a baby. If he were a teenage girl with a sister . . . well, I was one. And there were five of us. And I'm sure my mother fantasized about escaping, too."

"It's just the way Leila said it . . ."

"Everyone has their moments. Sometimes I feel like I

can't deal with this little guy for another second. It doesn't mean that I—"

"No, it doesn't mean that for you. But you're not Leila. And you're not missing."

Missing.

Molly considers the word. *Missing* isn't the same thing as not being where you're supposed to be. Well, technically it is, but missing has an ominous note to it.

She goes to her suitcase, unzips the compartment where she'd stashed her jewelry, and finds the necklace.

"September Girls," she says softly, turning over the pendant and gazing at the engraved letters. She puts the chain around her neck. Her hand trembles, and she fumbles with the clasp.

"Here, let me . . ." J.J. comes up behind her and fastens it.

"Thank you."

Molly turns to face her, struggling to maintain her composure. "We can't stay here. We're in the middle of nowhere, with smoke and fires and no phone service. We don't have a car, and we can't even call one."

"Shea's car is here. The Porsche, parked out front, and I know where the keys are."

"So do I, but we can't just steal a car, J.J. Anyway, the road is closed."

"How do we know that?"

"Because—"

"Because *he* said it's closed. The guy with the gun. We're going to trust that?"

They stare at each other.

"No." Molly shakes her head. "We're not going to trust him, or Shea. But we need to act like we do, until we figure out what happened to Leila and get out of here. Deal?"

"Deal. We need to go get my necklace and get back downstairs."

She unstraps Dawson and follows J.J. into the hall. They stop short, seeing Beck at the top of the stairs, as if he's been waiting for them.

"Everything okay, ladies?"

"I just had to change the baby," Molly lies. "But I found my necklace, see? I'm wearing it."

"And I'm going to grab mine. Be right down." J.J. hurries toward her room.

Beck gestures for Molly to precede him down the flight. She does, conscious of Beck's eyes on her, and of the gun he's carrying, its presence as tangible as the throbbing in her skull and the wind that hasn't let up since they got here.

Back in the library, she sees that Shea is looking at her phone.

"Is there service?" Molly asks.

"No. I keep checking. I tried to get a text out to Leila while we were by the water, because I had a signal, but then it disappeared. It looks like the text never went through."

Molly's heart sinks. "You mean it doesn't even work out there now?"

"It comes and goes."

Molly turns to Beck, trying not to sound accusatory. "You said you spoke to a utility worker yesterday. Shouldn't it be fixed by now?"

"I would have hoped so."

Dawson squirms and whines in her arms, as tired of being held as she is of holding him.

"Shh, it's okay, sweetie," she says, walking him around the room, from window to window. Outside, there's nothing to see but windy foliage and a smoky sky.

Footsteps scurry down the stairs.

J.J. appears. "It's not there. My necklace is gone."

SHEA

Shea puts a calming hand on J.J.'s arm. Her whole body is quaking.

"Are you sure it's not there?" Beck asks.

"I'm positive. I know exactly where it was."

Across the room, Molly sinks onto the couch. The baby reacts with a loud complaint, but she ignores him, holding him tightly on her lap as he wriggles.

"Is anything else missing?" Shea asks.

J.J. meets her gaze, and her pupils appear slightly dilated, as if she's in shock. She shakes her head. "I don't think so. I was just looking for the necklace. Someone came into my room and stole it from my bag."

Shea releases her grasp on J.J.'s arm. "Why don't you sit down? Would you like some water?"

"No, thank you." J.J. drops into the nearest chair, resting her forehead in her hands.

"When was the last time you saw it?" Beck asks. "Was it there this morning?"

She looks up. "This morning? No. I mean, I don't know if it was there. I didn't look for it until just now."

"Last night, then? You saw it last night?"

J.J. shakes her head, frowning. "At home. That's the last time I saw it. When I packed my bag."

"Then you might have accidentally left it behind?"

"No," she tells Beck firmly. "I brought it here. Leila wanted us all to wear them."

"But you didn't."

"I forgot." She nods at Molly, across the room. "We both forgot."

"Are we going to call the police?" Molly asks. "About the necklace, and Leila . . . I mean, shouldn't we call the police? Isn't that what you do when someone is missing?"

"I thought you have to wait twenty-four hours before you can report someone missing?" J.J. asks.

"With the phones down—" Beck begins, but Molly cuts him off.

"Can't we just go to the police station?"

"The road is closed."

Her mouth tightens. "Yes, you said. For the utility repairs. But they must let people through if there's an emergency. And a missing person is an emergency, right?"

"I'd say that depends on the circumstances. If Leila simply left the premises, and isn't endangered . . ." Shea watches the women carefully, gauging their reactions. Surely they've considered that scenario.

It's hard to tell. J.J. is stiff, hands clenched in her lap.

Molly is trying to extract the baby's hand from her long hair again.

Beck clears his throat. "The moment we report this, the situation becomes public knowledge and there's no going back. Your anonymity will have been compromised."

"Our *anonymity?*" Molly echoes. "That's what you're worried about?"

"There's been a lot of publicity surrounding the Dealin' Dice jackpot. The winner, or winners, become an instant target for the press, and for criminals. My role here is to help you prepare for that and establish protection for yourselves and your loved ones."

Seeing a look pass between the women, Shea jumps in. "I'm hoping, knowing Leila as well as you do, that you two may have some idea about whether she might have gone somewhere of her own accord."

"You mean, do we think she ran off without telling us, and stole J.J.'s necklace?" Molly asks. "That doesn't make sense."

"It makes sense when you consider that there's a billion dollars involved," Beck points out.

"But she has a family," Molly protests. "Two daughters. She wouldn't just leave them. That isn't like Leila, right, J.J.?"

"How do we know what is and isn't like Leila? Maybe this—whatever this is—maybe it's exactly like Leila."

"What do you mean?"

"A lot happens in twenty years." She shrugs. "People change. We don't know what Leila might do."

"What she'd *do*? You think she . . . *did* something?" she asks, as if J.J. just suggested Leila sprouted wings and flew to outer space. "Like what? What do you think?"

J.J. doesn't seem to have heard. Her fists are still clenched, and she's chewing her lower lip, avoiding eye contact.

"J.J.?" Shea asks. "What do you think?"

"About Leila? I don't know. I mean, I guess she's said some things that I wouldn't say. Or that you wouldn't say," she says, looking at Molly.

"About what?"

"Just that she wished she could get away from her daughters."

"But she didn't mean for good!" Molly says quickly. "She just meant . . . you know. They're teenagers. They're difficult."

"She said she doesn't miss them at all. I can't imagine saying that about my son."

"He's a grown man in the Marines."

"He's nineteen, Molly. He's a teenager."

"That's not the same thing." Molly turns to Shea. "Teenage girls are tough, especially on their moms. Do you have a sister?"

The question is a gut-slam.

Molly doesn't seem to notice or expect a reply. "I have four of them, so believe me, I get it. Having five teenage girls in the house was really hard on my mom, and she didn't even have a job. And she and my dad were together, and he did his share. Leila is juggling a lot, on her own. She's a good mom."

"She told us she's not," J.J. says. "She just told us she's a terrible mom."

"But we know she isn't."

"How can we know that? Really, how can we know anything about her life now? We haven't seen each other in years."

"We just saw each other last weekend."

"Molly, why are you trying so hard to protect Leila?"

"Why are *you* trying so hard to throw her under the bus?"

And there it is—the fissure Shea has seen in even the most rock-solid relationships once you introduce a vast amount of money.

"I'm not throwing her under the bus," J.J. says. "I'm being honest about what she said."

Molly turns to Shea. "Okay, so even if she's not supermom, that doesn't mean she ran off with a billion dollars."

"Of course it doesn't. We just have to consider all the scenarios and, unfortunately, that's one of them. Has she said anything else to make you think it's possible—or impossible—that she might do something like that?"

"She said that her family was getting on her nerves. She was laughing about how she wouldn't care if she never saw them again, and I . . ." J.J. crosses her arms, fists tucked under her elbows. "It made me uncomfortable. And Molly, too."

"I can speak for myself, J.J."

"So it didn't make you uncomfortable? To hear her talking about how she didn't care if she never saw her own children again?"

"She didn't say that! You're exaggerating."

Shea can understand why Molly would want to give her friend the benefit of the doubt. J.J., on the other hand, seems to be coming to terms with the idea that even loved ones are capable of unthinkable betrayal. Good for her. Life isn't nearly as complicated when you've accepted that reality.

"J.J., do you believe Leila's absence is an accident?" she asks.

After a pause, she says, "I don't know."

Molly rolls her eyes. "Oh, come on. Jumping to the conclusion that she stole a billion dollars and abandoned her family just because her kids have been getting on her nerves is like saying an alien spaceship must be blocking out the sun, when there could be a million other explanations, like clouds or smoke, or . . ."

"That's not a million other explanations," J.J. points out. "She literally just told us yesterday that she's good at leaving people and not looking back."

Beck's eyebrows shoot up. "What do you mean?"

"Leila's been estranged from her family for years now."

"But that's different," Molly says.

"How? Could you turn your back on your parents and sisters, Molly? Walk away and never look back?"

"No, but I wasn't abandoned by my own mother—not even once, but twice."

"What do you mean?" Shea asks.

"For one thing, Leila's birth mother gave her up for adoption and never looked for her, and—"

"Okay, but the same thing happened to me," J.J. cuts in.

"What? No, it didn't. You weren't adopted."

"No, but I never knew my father. My mother got pregnant at sixteen, and he was never in my life."

"That's different," Molly says. "You don't even know if she told him she was pregnant. Anyway, we're not talking about your father. We're talking about Leila's birth mother. And her adoptive parents."

"What happened with them?" Shea asks.

"They were estranged. Leila decided not to become a doctor like they wanted her to. They cut her off and cut her out of their lives. She found out her mother died years ago and her father and brothers never even told her. She always felt alienated because she was adopted. The brothers were the parents' biological children. Anyway, J.J. and I were there for her when she went through all that. And she's always been a loyal friend to both of us."

"Has she, though?"

"Of course she has."

"What about Stef Kiley?"

Molly's blue eyes narrow. "She was a friend to him, too."

"You know that's not what I mean."

"Who's Stef Kiley?" Shea asks.

"He lived across the hall from us in college," Molly says. "We were all part of a big group."

"And Stef was Molly's boyfriend. She told me and Leila that she was going to marry him, and then Leila—"

"That's ancient history! Why are you even bringing it up?"

"Because we're talking about what kind of friend Leila's

been to you. And what kind of person she is. What she's capable of."

"Fooling around with your college roommate's boy- friend doesn't have much to do with who you are twenty years later, J.J."

"Unless you're still doing it."

"Doing what?"

J.J. just looks at Molly, as if she's waiting for her to fig- ure it out.

Molly frowns. "What are you saying?"

"Never mind." J.J. stands and heads for the door.

"Wait, where are you going?"

"For a walk. I need to clear my head." She leaves the room without another word or backward glance.

J.J.

Somehow, J.J. had forgotten the fires and the wind and being trapped here until she stepped outside. Now reality
slams her and she looks with longing at the Porsche Boxster
parked by the tiled veranda. It's Shea's, parked here since
last night, and she'd seen the keys hanging on a hook inside.
It would be so easy to grab them and flee.

But is she really going to leave Molly and the baby here
with an armed stranger? Especially now?

She never should have told Molly about Stef.

She wasn't planning on it—certainly not now, and not
this way—but somehow, it came tumbling out of her.

A person can only keep so many secrets.

Leila had confessed this one late last night, after Molly
had gone to bed. Why hadn't J.J. gone up to bed, too? She'd
already had too much to drink, and on the heels of that
medication. But Leila persuaded her to linger for a nightcap.

That part is fuzzy.

She remembers more gin. So much gin, far too much gin.

She doesn't remember how she and Leila had ended

up outside on pool loungers, sharing a cigarette, but she does remember that Leila not only didn't mind that J.J. still smokes, but had confessed to sneaking one now and then herself.

"Don't tell Molly," J.J. remembers saying. "She won't like it."

Later—how much later?—Leila had said the same thing, about her renewed relationship with Stef. "Don't tell Molly."

J.J. had promised that she wouldn't, and she'd intended to honor that—not to protect Leila, but for Molly's sake. Because even in her inebriated state, J.J. had known that nothing good would ever come of her finding out.

So why the hell did you just tell her?

Because despite everything, Molly persists in believing the best about Leila? The best about everyone? Including J.J.

She tries to suck air deeply and rhythmically into her lungs, as Dr. Michaels had suggested she do when she's feeling anxious.

Breathe. In . . . out . . . in . . . out . . .

A panic attack can trigger your fight-or-flight instinct . . .

The perception of danger isn't grounded in reality . . .

Use your breathing exercises to control your anxiety . . .

She does her best.

Inhale and hold it . . . one, two, three . . . exhale . . .

Yeah, maybe that works when you're not surrounded by fire. The smoke is getting to her again. Every breath infuses her body with the toxic reminder of everything that's gone so horribly wrong, of being trapped here for God knows how much longer.

She can't just stand here. She has to do something.

Something that isn't stealing that car and fleeing without Molly and Dawson.

She hurries away, around the side of the house, toward the path that leads out to the water.

Her phone will work there. She needs to hear John's voice. It will ground her, as always, reminding her of who she is. Or at least, who she used to be, before all this—before Leila, before the panic and depression, before she'd lost her job, before John, even . . .

She walks, and she remembers, and somehow it's all so clear, all the way back to when she was a little girl.

She and her mom, Carolyn, had lived with J.J.'s grandparents for the first five years of her life, while Carolyn worked as a waitress and finished high school at night.

J.J. can still see the house, a small, vinyl-sided ranch with a plastic Virgin Mary grotto out front and painted crucifixes with bloody Jesuses hanging in every room. She can see her grandfather, silent and endlessly sitting in front of the television. He watched only sitcoms, all night, every night. Ironic, that her childhood evenings had been punctuated by laugh tracks, but her grandfather never once cracked a smile.

Far more indelible in J.J.'s memory is the dour grandmother who'd never forgiven the anonymous boy who'd impregnated her only daughter, nor her daughter for allowing it to happen, nor her granddaughter for existing.

Once, J.J. had asked her grandmother about her father, and she'd reacted with such fury that J.J. never brought it up with her again.

Back in college, Leila had urged her to get the details from her mother and was incredulous when J.J. said she had no interest in him.

It wasn't entirely true. Of course she was curious. Still is. But she resented Leila's attitude. It was as if J.J. was shirking some noble duty.

"I can't believe you, J.J.! At the very least, you owe it to yourself to find out. I mean, think of how it makes me feel that you can easily get information and aren't doing it!"

"What you're saying, then, is that I owe you?"

She was being sardonic, but Leila responded with a vigorous nod.

"Yes! Me, and other adoptees who would literally kill to have the slightest lead."

"You do realize that by saying you'd literally kill, you mean you would . . ."

"Literally kill. Right. Yes. That's how desperate I am to know about my biological family."

"Well, if I ever get any intel on *your* birth father, Leila, I promise you'll be the first to know. But you already have two parents who love you, and three brothers, too. That's more than I'll ever have."

Conception was the only role her birth father had ever played in her life. Carolyn was the one who'd been there for her; the one who'd dreamed big dreams for her daughter; the one who'd taught J.J. that anything was possible as long as she got good grades and won scholarships to a good college and worked hard and saved all her money.

She'd believed in all that, believed in herself, until she lost her mother. That had been the turning point; the moment when everything started falling apart.

And now look. Look what's become of her. Look where she is.

"*You* did this," she says aloud, and the words are lost in the sound of the wind and the crashing waves in the distance.

Then she hears another voice. "*You* did this!"

An echo of her own?

Or is someone out here with her?

She glances back at the house, filmy behind a haze of smoke, made filmier because she's so nearsighted without her glasses.

She thinks about the figure Molly had claimed to see, and about the bump on Molly's head, and about Chantal Charbonneau, missing twenty years, and about Shea, who'd known her, and Beck, with the gun, and Leila.

"Dammit, Leila. Damn you."

The hot wind snatches the words from her lips, and she hurries on, reaching into the pocket of her sweatshirt for her phone and the pack of cigarettes and matches she'd grabbed before leaving her room.

She hadn't dared linger upstairs to steal a smoke before reporting the necklace missing, but oh, how she'd longed for one. Now the need is fierce.

She thrusts a cigarette into her mouth and looks around

for a sheltered spot where she can get a match, out of this wind. Spotting a small shed across a clearing, she branches off in that direction. She's nearly there when her phone suddenly vibrates in her hand.

Checking it, she sees that it has a weak signal. There are no new texts, but she's missed a call. No, three calls, from . . .

The bank.

Really?

She scurries to the side of the shed, presses John's number on autodial, and props the phone between her shoulder and ear so that she can light a cigarette.

The match goes out once, twice, three times.

The phone rings once, twice, three times.

The fourth match stays lit long enough for her to hold the flame to the tip of the cigarette and inhale deeply as the call bounces to the familiar recording.

"I can't take your call right now, but if you leave a message, I'll get back to you as soon as possible."

She clears her throat, and his name emerges on a sob. "John? John, I need—"

She breaks off as a creaking sound pushes past her own voice and the pulse pounding in her ears.

A creaking sound. As if someone just opened the door on the opposite side of the shed.

It's followed by footsteps, rustling through tall grass, running, running away.

She peers around the side of the shed, just in time to see a woman disappear into the trees.

MOLLY

Stef.

Stef . . . and Leila? Again?

Even now, the thought of them together makes Molly's gut twist.

After J.J. dropped that bombshell and fled, Molly had excused herself, saying she had to take Dawson back upstairs to change him.

"I thought you just did that?" Beck asked.

"Oh, I did. I mean . . . I have to feed him."

At least that was a partial truth. She doesn't necessarily *have* to feed him just yet, but Dawson is happy to get off her lap and into the high chair, even if strained broccoli isn't his favorite.

Spooning green goo into his mouth, Molly allows her thoughts to wander back to September 2000. She, Leila, and J.J. had three tickets to see the Bangles at the House of Blues in Chicago, where the band would be sure to play their hit cover of Big Star's "September Gurls"—the perfect September Girls birthday celebration.

But J.J. couldn't find anyone to cover her shift at the campus dining hall that night, and Molly was sick in bed that night with what felt like a bad case of strep throat.

It had been her idea to give Stef her ticket to go with Leila.

"Come on, sweetie," she tells Dawson when he seals his lips and turns away from the spoon. "Just two more bites and then you'll be done. Yummy broccoli. Yummy . . ."

She'd thought nothing of it when Leila, always squeamish about germs, kept her distance in the days that followed. When her strep throat turned out to be mono, she'd joked to Leila and J.J., "At least you guys don't have to worry. They call it 'the kissing disease,' and I haven't been kissing you. But Stef is probably going to get it."

He had.

Maybe she should have been suspicious when Leila, too, came down with mono. Especially when Leila went into a tremendous amount of scientific detail about how it was spread by saliva, not just kissing, and she herself could have gotten it from sharing a toothbrush holder or maybe sipping from Molly's drink.

Of course, that was all true, biologically speaking. Molly had just never considered that Leila might also have been kissing Stef at the concert that night—and doing more than kissing.

Their friendship had survived the crisis, though her relationship with Stef had not. She probably wouldn't think twice about any of this now if not for—

"Dawson, no!"

Too late. He pushes down on the spoon she's holding out and then lets go, catapulting green puree all over Molly and the wall behind her.

"Message received, kid. You're fed up with broccoli."

She cleans Dawson and the wall, but it'll take more than a damp wipe to clean the goo clumped in her blond hair.

"Mommy will be right back," she tells him, and leaves him strapped in the high chair with a couple of toys. With the bathroom door open so that she can peek at him, she takes the world's fastest shower in the claw-foot tub, using the handheld spray nozzle and missing the walk-in marble rain shower at her own house.

Well, Ross's house, and her days there are numbered. Having transitioned from imminent homelessness to "money is no object," she refuses to entertain the idea that her best friend just stole her salvation.

That money ensures that she'll never have to worry about her child's future, or her ex husband's place in it. He won't be a part of Dawson's life in any way.

As it is, his role is strictly financial. He's obligated to provide child support, same as he does with his daughters. But for his son, there will be nothing more. He'd assured Molly of that from the moment she refused to terminate the pregnancy.

Painful as that was, she knew even back then that it would probably be for the best.

But Ross could always change his mind. As much as Molly's own father adores his girls, he'd always wanted a boy—maybe not instead, but in addition. Ross might eventually decide to forge a relationship with Dawson after all. Or Dawson might one day seek out his father.

Things will unfold very differently if Molly can afford to raise him without Ross's money.

But what if Leila really did take off with that winning ticket?

Or if something terrible really has happened to her?

Had a masked intruder barged in and taken her away at gunpoint? Is she, at this very moment, bound and gagged and locked in the trunk of a car that's taking her farther and farther away? Is she begging for her life?

Am I next?

"Stop, Molly!" she mutters, pulling on a fluffy white robe and wrapping a towel around her wet hair.

Leila will turn up in one piece, and they'll cash in the ticket, and everything will be fine.

But for now, she's going to stay right where she is, locked in this suite with her baby, safe even if someone really is creeping around the house. Not a ghost, or hallucination.

She leans into the bathroom mirror to study the angry red bump on her forehead.

What if she really does have a concussion? What if she imagined that open door and a person sneaking out of the room? Or what if she got knocked out last night and everything that's happened since is just a crazy dream, like Dorothy in Oz?

She closes her eyes, willing herself back, not to Kansas but to yesterday, when she was with her September Girls, celebrating their extraordinarily good fortune.

It doesn't work. She's still here, and it's still now. Go figure.

She leaves the bathroom. Dawson is fussing in the high chair, having tossed every toy overboard. She picks him up, but he isn't in the mood to be held, which is fine with her.

She puts a quilt on the floor and sits him in the middle, surrounded by enough interactive toys to keep him entertained for a while.

Molly needs something to take her mind off the situation, at a loss without the internet, television, or even a book other than the one on her nightstand about the "*hot dry Santa Anas that come down through the mountain passes and curl your hair and make your nerves jump and your skin itch.*"

She checks her phone in case a cell signal has magically appeared so that she'll be able to call for help, or call her mother, who must be worried sick by now, or even call Leila.

Yes, and Leila will answer and tell Molly that everything's fine, that she just went for a walk off the property and the utility workers wouldn't let her back up.

The scenario calms Molly for a few moments. Then she remembers what Leila had said about her daughters, and what J.J. had told her about Stef, and the shadowy figure that had slipped out of Chantal's room.

This isn't a dream, and it isn't Oz.

This is a house where women disappear, and—

She remembers the podcast—something she can do with her phone that doesn't require cellular service or Wi-Fi.

After quickly dressing and combing through her damp

hair, she settles in a chair and opens the podcast app. Realizing that she'd inadvertently downloaded every season of *Disappearing Acts*, she scrolls her library, scanning the episode descriptions for Chantal's name.

Midway through season two, a different one jumps out at her.

Intrigued, Molly puts on her earbuds, leans back, and presses Play.

SHEA

Left alone with Beck in the library, Shea asks in a low voice, "Well? Which do you think it is? Did someone abduct Leila Randolph? Or did she run off with the ticket?"

"If she was going to keep the money for herself and run away, she didn't even have to bother telling her friends they'd won. She could have just cashed in the ticket and taken off."

"They'd have figured it out sooner or later. They chose meaningful numbers together," Shea points out. "Plus, it's been all over the news the last few days. Everyone knows exactly where the winning ticket was sold."

"Okay, so she couldn't keep it from them. But if she was planning to cheat them out of their share, why bother hiring Windfall, flying the others out to California, coming to the house?"

"Maybe she had good intentions at first, but something happened to make her change her mind."

"Sounds like you don't think it was foul play."

Again, she thinks of the cupola, less certain now that

Leila had been the interloper. Still, some instinctive lack of trust keeps her from sharing it with him.

"Well, now that we know she's been estranged from her parents and brothers for twenty-odd years, I find it easier to believe she might be capable of leaving her daughters behind."

"And running off with an old flame, and stealing a billion dollars from her best friends?"

Shea shrugs. "She might be. Or, the best friends might be involved in this. I feel like they're not being completely honest with us?"

"And with each other. If I had internet access, I'd be checking into all three backgrounds right now."

"I can have Justin do that. I'll go out to where I can get a cell signal and call him right now." She heads for the door.

"Good idea. I'll come with you."

"Why?"

"Because you shouldn't be out there alone when we don't know what's going on here."

"I'm a big girl, Beck. I've been alone for years. Even when I wasn't," she throws back over her shoulder, and exits the house before he can comment or come after her.

Outside, she follows the path toward the sea, shaking her head as if she might dislodge Beck from her brain. No luck. He'd velcroed himself there from Day One.

Day One—five years ago, she'd interviewed him to travel with a new client. He'd looked good on paper—former military Special Forces, working the past few years on covert protection detail, and of course experienced with UHNWI.

He looked good in person, too, when he walked into her office—tall, dark, and square jawed, lean and muscular in a well-cut suit. Their eyes met and held as they shook hands, and she knew he was trouble.

She hired him anyway, telling herself that it wasn't as if she, personally, needed to have direct contact with him . . .

Except, she *needed* to have direct contact with him. Needed it in the worst way.

But she doesn't want to remember that now.

The breakup—if you can even call it a breakup—had blindsided them both, even Shea, though she'd initiated it and it had been a long time coming. Their relationship—if you can call it that—had been on-again, off-again for years. But she'd known that this particular off-again would be permanent.

It has been; will continue to be.

As soon as they figure out what happened to Leila Randolph and he can get out of here . . . out of her house, her thoughts, her life.

J.J.

For a long time, J.J. just stands by the shed and smokes, lighting a second cigarette from the first and staring at the spot where the woman had disappeared. It helps a little—the soothing rhythm of inhaling, exhaling, sucking nicotine deeply into her lungs.

The figure had been blurred by her nearsightedness—slight and quick, with long hair whipping in the wind.

She tosses the last cigarette to the ground and grinds it out with her shoe, then walks around to the shed door.

It's ajar, just as the balcony door had been.

J.J. gives it a push and it creaks open. The interior is dim, but there's a bare bulb in the middle of the space with a string pull hanging down. She steps in and gives it a yank, illuminating the shed.

She sees landscaping equipment and stacked garden furniture. A white cell phone charger is plugged into an outlet, without a phone attached. A wrought-iron chair and small table separate from the rest, as if someone had been sitting there. There's a crumpled protein bar wrapper on the table, the same brand she'd seen in a jar in the kitchen. She'd helped herself to one earlier—or had that been last night?

She has a vague memory of rummaging through the cabinets with Leila, looking for a midnight snack. Was that before or after they'd gone out to smoke by the pool?

There's an open diet soda can on the floor beside the chair. She notices ashes flecked on top of the can, and when she lifts it, she sees—and smells—soggy cigarette butts in what's left of the liquid.

It could have been left behind by a worker.

Or by the woman she'd seen.

A woman who smokes.

MOLLY

"*By the time she disappeared in 2001, she was living in isolation at Windfall, a seaside estate north of Los Angeles,*" Riley Robertson is saying, as Molly stands in front of the fireplace staring at the painting of the woman on the cliff.

"*The general consensus is that she's dead—that she either jumped, fell, or was pushed to her death and her body was swallowed by the sea. That makes sense, right?*"

"It does to me," Molly says aloud.

And to Riley Robertson, who answers her own question, "*Sure it does. And we're going to examine that theory. We're also going to consider a far more intriguing one. What if she staged her disappearance in order to escape the spotlight and live out her days in obscurity?*"

Hearing a sharp bang, Molly quickly presses Pause and pulls out one of the earbuds. She can hear the wind, and Dawson is contentedly playing with a jingly toy.

Then she hears it again, and realizes it's a loud knock on the door.

She hurries over and is about to unlock it but thinks better.

"Who is it?"

"J.J.!"

She slides the bolt and opens the door.

"Molly!" J.J. clutches a hand to her chest as if she's having a heart attack.

"What's wrong? Are you okay?"

"I am now." J.J. steps into the room and reaches back to close the door and lock it. "I've been knocking and knocking and I thought you were gone, too!"

"Sorry." Molly pulls out the other earbud and shows them to J.J. "I was just listening to that podcast and you'll never believe what I—"

"I saw her, Molly."

She gasps "Leila?"

"No! I mean . . . I don't know. I was outside, trying to find a signal so that I could call John, and I saw a woman come out of a shed and she disappeared before I could—"

"A ghost? You saw a ghost. I knew this place was haunted. I can feel it."

"No, it wasn't a ghost! She didn't vanish into thin air. She *ran*. Like she didn't want me to see her. Like what you saw, this morning."

Molly nods, remembering the figure she'd seen emerge from Chantal's room.

"What did she look like?"

"I don't know. I only saw her from the back. She had long hair."

"Could it have been Leila?"

J.J. hesitates. "Yes. It could have been."

She crosses the room and sits on the bed.

Molly sits beside her. "Or maybe it was Chantal."

"Maybe." J.J. looks at the phone and earbuds Molly's holding. "You were listening to the podcast? You said there was something that I wouldn't believe?"

"Oh—right. Remember that memorial marker Leila saw by the water? With the quote by Antoine de Saint-Exupéry?"

"Yes."

"He disappeared, too, J.J."

"What do you mean?"

"I accidentally downloaded previous seasons of the podcast, and I saw his name in the description for an episode about writers who've vanished. I listened to it . . . I mean, not all of it. I fast-forwarded through a lot. But it turns out this Antoine went missing in 1944."

"And . . . ?"

"And, don't you think it's a coincidence? That Chantal's marker has a quote by this French guy who disappeared just like she did?"

"That was, what? At least fifteen years before Chantal was even born, Molly. It's not as if she knew him."

"No, but don't you see? It's a clue."

"Now you sound like Leila."

Molly shrugs and starts to get up. "Okay, well, I just thought it might be—"

"I'm sorry," J.J. says quickly, putting a hand on her arm.

"You're right. It might be a clue. I'm just freaked out about seeing that person, and . . . I owe you an apology, Molly."

"It's okay. I freaked out when I saw her, too."

"No, not for that. For . . . you know. What I said about Leila. And Stef."

Molly stiffens. "Is it true?"

"Yes."

"How long have you known?"

"Only since last night. After you went to bed, we stayed up for a while, and she told me."

"Why didn't she tell me?" she asks J.J. "And why didn't you?"

"She asked me not to."

Molly winces. "Wow. Seriously? It's not as if I've even seen Stef since college. So Leila being back with him isn't a big deal to me."

"Well, she's not really back with him. I mean, she was, but she says it's over because he wouldn't leave Heidi."

"Heidi? His wife?" Molly asks, as if she doesn't know. As if lies aren't flying out of her.

"Right. Leila said they have this perfect life, and his wife is the main breadwinner. And—remember, she was drunk, and so was I, but basically what she said was that she was hoping he'd reconsider now that she has all this money."

"Let me get this straight. Leila told you she wants to *buy* him out of his marriage?"

"Not in those words."

"But that's the gist of it, right?"

"It's . . . yes," J.J. admits, with obvious reluctance.

"Wow. Shame on her for trying. And shame on him if he goes for it. I feel sorry for his wife."

"Maybe she knew exactly what kind of man she was marrying. She's no fool, with an Ivy League MBA and high-powered corporate career."

"Leila told you that?"

"Yes."

"I wonder why she married him, though."

"Maybe she just loved him. Isn't that the usual reason?"

Molly shrugs. "I'm sure it was for you, with John. From the moment you met him, you were crazy about him."

"I'm sure you were the same way with Ross."

"It's hard to say. When I met him, my father was sick and I was a little lost, and—" She shakes her head. "We're not talking about me. Or you. We're talking about Stef."

Stef freaking Kiley. Molly shakes her head.

He was never the best-looking man in the world, though he's handsome enough, with dark hair and eyes and a broad-shouldered build. Nor is he the smartest, despite a sharp sense of humor and a decent GPA.

But he's by far the most charismatic, seductive . . . and soulless.

Molly stands and paces across the room. Dawson drops his toy and holds out his arms, wanting to be picked up.

"In a minute, sweetie," she says, and turns back to see that J.J. is holding her phone. "Hey—is service back?"

"No. I keep checking."

"Did you get ahold of John?"

"Hmm?"

"You said that's what you were trying to do when you saw our mystery woman out there."

"Oh. Right. No, he's at work. I got his voice mail."

Dawson is whining now. She bends over and hands him a toy, asking J.J., "Did you leave him a message?"

She shrugs. "It's not like I can have him call me back."

"But you can tell him about Leila, and see if he thinks we should call the police, and help us figure out what we should do and how we can get out of here."

"He's two thousand miles away, Molly. And if I leave him a message telling him any of that, and he can't get in touch with me, he's going to freak out. I can't do that to him."

"No, of course you can't. Sorry. I'm just . . ."

Just hoping for someone else's husband to come to her rescue? For any man to rescue her?

"I guess I'll do anything not to have to handle a problem on my own, huh?"

Dawson throws the toy as if to punctuate that and strains his arms toward her.

"What do you mean?"

"It's what I do. What I've always done. My father. Stef. Ross. Life is so much easier when you get to lean on someone. On a *man*. And they've all let me down. Except my dad . . . until he got sick and I realized he was a mere mortal."

She picks up the baby and meets J.J.'s gaze over his head.

"I know that was hard on you, Molly, when your dad got sick. I went through that with my mom."

"It was. It was—" She catches herself. "But it wasn't

harder than losing a mom and never having a dad at all. I'm so sorry, J.J. I didn't mean to sound so callous about that before, when I said your father might not even know you exist."

Something hardens in J.J.'s eyes. "It's okay. It's probably true."

"But it was insensitive. I was just trying to prove a point about Leila."

"I know."

"I really didn't mean to—"

"Molly! It's fine! Please drop it." She stands, rubbing her temple.

"Are you okay?"

"I just have a headache."

"Go rest."

"I guess I might as well since we're just stuck here. We—" She stops, shaking her head, eyes bleak, and repeats, "We're stuck here."

"Do you want to do something? We can try—"

"No, Molly. Right now, there's nothing I want to do, or try. Okay? I just need to rest, like you said."

Molly closes the door after her, then quietly slides the old-fashioned iron bolt across it.

She looks down at Dawson. He meets her gaze with his big blue eyes and regrets churn in her brain. She should have left him with her parents; should have told them the truth; should never have come here in the first place; shouldn't have allowed Leila to bring Windfall into their lives.

Leila . . . where are you?

She needs Leila to be *here*, dammit.

Molly needs that money. It's the only way she'll be able to take care of her child and herself, from here on in.

If it falls through—if Leila really did take off with the ticket—then Molly will be right back where she started, dependent on Ross, and her parents, for the rest of her—

Wait a minute.

Money will solve her financial problems and change a lot of other things about her situation, but it won't change who she is. She didn't earn it. It fell into her lap.

Yeah, well, what was she supposed to do about that? Turn it down, like some noble . . . idiot? No one in her right mind would walk away from a vast fortune.

Or would she?

She glances again at the painting of the woman on the cliff.

The most plausible theory is that she just ran away and took on a new identity, Leila's voice reminds her.

It was so Leila of her, to be so unequivocal about a mystery no one else in the world had ever been able to solve.

And now she, too, has vanished.

Not just vanished, but vanished from the exact same spot.

That's some coincidence, Molly thinks.

Unless it isn't.

SHEA

Shea sees Chantal on the cliff high above the sea. Not the woman, and not a ghost, but a memory. She isn't preparing to jump, but is staring out at the sea and longing to transport herself across it to a place where she can make a fresh start.

In her mind's eye, Chantal becomes Leila, standing in the same precarious spot, contemplating the same thing.

And then, what? She'd staged her suicide with a necklace she'd stolen from J.J.? Why would she have done that? Because she couldn't bear to part with her own, wanting to keep it as a souvenir of her old life and the friends she'd double-crossed?

That makes no sense.

Unless she'd stolen J.J.'s necklace yesterday, and it was the one she'd been wearing? Maybe she'd forgotten her own at home. Maybe . . .

But that doesn't make sense, either. There are other things she could have used to stage the scene.

A sound permeates the wind and waves—a rustling on

the path behind her. She whirls around, expecting to see Beck. Of course he'd followed her out here, the he-man trying to protect the little woman.

But there's no Beck.

There's no one.

Keeping her eye on the path, Shea pulls her phone out of her pocket and is relieved to see that she has service. She quickly calls Justin.

He answers on the first ring. "There you are! I've been trying to reach you."

"There's no service unless I'm out by the water, and even then, it comes and goes. What's going on? How's Abi? Did you go to the funeral?"

"Yes. It was rough. He's struggling."

She nods.

Facing a future without a loved one changes everything. It changes who and what you are and how the world sees you.

Same as facing a future with a vast fortune.

The bereaved and the newly wealthy are opposite sides of the same coin. When life irrevocably changes overnight, for better or worse, you need to digest and adjust to the new reality. Saying goodbye to the past—even past imperfect—takes a great deal of energy as well as time.

"Listen, Shea, I've been following the news, and there are a couple of new fires east of Windfall. They're closing roads all around you."

"I know, Beck said they're making repairs."

"I think you should get out of there."

"You're cutting in and out, Justin. I might lose you."

"I said, get out of—"

"I heard that. But it's not that simple. Leila Randolph is missing."

"*Missing?* What do you mean?"

"She was here last night, and this morning she was gone."

"Did you look for her?"

"Nah, we decided not to bother."

"What? Shea, that's—"

"Of course we looked for her! We searched every inch of the house, and the grounds. She's nowhere to be found."

"Do you think something happened to her?"

"That, or she took off with the ticket."

She quickly fills him in on the rest of the story—about Leila's rekindled affair with the college flame, her recent comments about wanting to get away from her life, and the fact that she's been estranged from her parents for two decades.

"I've been estranged from my parents for twice as long," Justin says. "I'm sure she had her reasons, just like I had mine."

"Her friends say the parents wanted her to follow in their career footsteps."

"And my parents wanted me to follow in their heterosexuality footsteps. Did you call the police?"

"Not yet. It's only been a few hours."

"How about her boyfriend and her daughters? Have you checked in with them?"

"Not yet," she says again. "I'm not sure that's a good idea just yet, but can you please find the contact info for the boyfriend and ex-husband?"

"Sure."

"And I also need you to do some sniffing around online. See what you can find out about them and Leila's life, her friends' lives, and this Stef person."

"'Stef person' isn't a lot to go on."

"His last name is Kiley, and he went to Northwestern with the others. See if you can find out where he is, and whether her boyfriend and daughters are where they're supposed to be. Especially the daughters. Maybe she didn't leave them behind. Maybe they're with her."

"But wouldn't she have just run, if she was going to? Why go to Windfall?"

"Because it's Windfall. Leila knew Chantal's story. She was snooping around the house and asking questions about her last night. I think she was doing her homework and getting ready to cover her tracks. Showing up at the house and going through the motions made everyone assume that something horrible happened to her."

"As opposed to assuming that she *did* something horrible."

"Well, yes. There's only one problem with any of this," Shea tells him. "Lottery winners can stay anonymous in some states, but California isn't one of them."

"She still could have taken off with the ticket. Maybe

she wants to establish herself somewhere else and then she'll claim the money."

"Maybe you should back off looking for her."

"I'll do that if you'll do something for me," he says.

"What is it?"

"Get out of there before it gets dangerous."

"I will, Justin, as soon as I find out what happened to Leila. She's my responsibility and—"

"Shea—"

"—and people don't just vanish into thin air."

"Chantal did."

"Well, I'll go if we're evacuated."

"You will be, any second now."

"Then I'll go *when* we're evacuated."

"What about the others?" he asks. "I can arrange for them to be picked up. J.J. and Molly and the baby. And the dogs."

"You forgot Beck."

"I didn't forget him, but he's not going anywhere until you do."

She stiffens. "What makes you say that? He's not my . . . my . . ." She settles on, "Bodyguard."

"He's like the captain of a ship. He's not leaving until all the passengers are safe."

"You've got it backward, Justin. Beck is the passenger here. Windfall is *my* ship, and *I'm* the captain. Anyway, you don't have to send a car. He's got one. He can drive everyone back to LA."

His reply is lost in a crackle of static.

"Justin? Justin?"

His voice is scrambled.

"I'm losing you," she calls. "I'll be back in touch later to see what you've found out."

She hangs up, uncertain whether he heard her.

J.J.

J.J.'s room is at the front of the house, overlooking the front drive and a Porsche Boxster that's still parked by the door.

She stares at the car and smokes a cigarette, exhaling through the open casement window, feeling like a prisoner trapped in a tower cell awaiting execution.

She's been trying to focus on the woman in the shed and Chantal and Leila. But, for reasons that have nothing to do with losing her glasses, the distant past is sharper than what happened just yesterday.

And so she thinks about that. About Molly. About the night she'd found out about Leila and Stef the first time. She doesn't recall where she was when the confrontation began. Probably in the library or working her job as a dining hall cashier.

It was late when she returned to the dorm—after dark and snowing. The windows were closed, yet she remembers hearing distraught wailing even before she entered the building. She didn't know it was coming from her own room, and she thought something terrible must have happened to someone. A death in the family, maybe, or a failed midterm.

On her floor, all the doors along the corridor were propped open. That wasn't unusual. People were always blasting music, shouting back and forth, hanging out in the halls or drifting between each other's rooms.

But in her memory, that night was preternaturally quiet aside from the sobs, as if everyone was trying to hear what was going on behind the door marked forty-six. It was closed, as was the one across the hall, where Stef lived.

J.J. never knew whether Stef was there that night, listening, or if he'd had the good fortune to be out. Or maybe he'd heard it start to unfold and fled. That wouldn't have surprised her at all. No, that would have been right on brand.

All she knows for sure is that when she walked in, Molly was a crumpled, soggy heap on her bed, and Leila was pacing.

"What happened?" J.J. dropped her backpack and went to Molly. "Did someone—"

"I slept with Stef," Leila announced.

It was so very Leila, the way she owned it, issuing a matter-of-fact statement and no apology. Not to J.J., anyway.

To Molly, she apologized profusely. To her credit, she didn't blame it on having too much to drink, or on Stef seducing her, or on her emotional instability on the heels of dropping premed and becoming estranged from her family.

"I'd never want to hurt you in a million years, Molly," she said, crouched on the floor at Molly's side, handing her tissues. "If I could go back in time and change things, I would. But I can't. I can only go forward, and if you can accept my apology and get past this, I promise I'll be the best friend you could ever have, for the rest of our lives."

"I'll try. He was just a boyfriend, but you're my friend. And that's what friends do, right? They forgive each other."

Molly had forgiven Leila back then.

And now?

She acted as though the rekindled affair is no big deal, but J.J. isn't convinced she was being completely honest. Something feels off, but . . .

Molly is her friend. They know each other. Trust each other.

At least, they *did* know and trust each other, years ago.

But so much has changed. Decades have passed since they shared a dorm, or even a time zone.

Molly claimed she doesn't care about Leila and Stef, but for a trained actress, Molly is a terrible liar.

But then, so is J.J.

She hears Leila's voice in her head, echoing back from last weekend. "Tell me everything!"

And Molly's. "How's work going?"

J.J. could have stopped her right there. She was supposed to share her truth with her friends. She and Dr. Michaels had practiced. She'd start small, but eventually, she'd get to that awful wee-hour December phone call and the rest, all of it.

"I lost my job," she was going to say, or better yet, "I was fired."

It's the truth after all. Fired in a voice mail.

To be fair, her supervisor probably would have done it in person if J.J. had shown up in the office that morning. Or that week.

Then again, if J.J. had made it there, she never would have gotten fired at all.

Day after day, instead of getting up and going to work, she had stayed in bed. She hadn't bothered to call in sick or tell her colleagues what was going on. She'd just checked herself out of the situation, same as she had the first time, with the postpartum depression.

She hears John's voice in her head, laced with concern. "What's going on with you, babe? Please talk to me."

"I just needed to hear your voice," she whispers, turning away from the window and looking down at her phone, sheathed in a protective blue case John had bought for her after she'd dropped it and cracked the screen. It's one hundred percent shatterproof. Too bad they don't make them for human hearts.

She can hear John telling her not to worry—that everything is all right, and he'll do whatever he can to help her from wherever he is.

Or, better yet, he'll tell her that he's already here with her.

"But how is that possible?" she'll ask.

"Open the door," he'll respond, and when she opens it, there he'll be, just like in the movies.

A fierce ache pushes into her throat.

John will sweep her into his sturdy embrace and promise her that everything's going to be okay, despite the lost fortune and Leila and that shadowy woman and the shed and the fires burning all around them and the wind, that damned devil wind, not letting up for a moment.

She returns to the window, about to light another cigarette when she realizes that the Porsche is gone.

SHEA

Shea retraces her steps, away from the water.

This time the wind isn't behind her, thrusting her forward. Now it's coming right at her, as if trying to hold her back from the house.

She keeps on going and thinks of Corey, who'd taken her own life on a grim March day at the tail end of rainy season.

Sometimes, Shea thinks that if the weather had been better, her sister would still be alive. She'd always loved to be outdoors on a beautiful day, even in the old neighborhood where all you could do was sit around on the stoop, and you had to come in before dark, when the dealers took over the block.

Corey never touched drugs back then. Such bitter irony. It wasn't until they moved out of the city and up in the world that she started running with the fast crowd.

Deep down, Shea knows it would have taken more than warm sunshine to save Corey's life. She was an addict, so far gone by the time she OD'd that she no longer came home at night or rarely ever; no longer tucked her little sister safely into bed.

May the dreams you hold dearest be those that come true . . .

Shea's father had broken the devastating news that day when she came home from school. He'd used the word "gone," as if he couldn't bear to say "dead."

She remembers running from the house into cold rain and wind, and waves crashing far below, and a bird . . .

She shoves away the memory.

She doesn't believe in curses. Not the paranormal kind, anyway. She believes—she's *certain*—that human beings create their own misfortune.

But maybe that's what she's been doing, clinging to this remnant of her past and its secrets under the guise of convenience. There are other remote locations she can adapt to her business needs; places where she won't be haunted by what might have been, and the ghosts of all the souls she's lost—lost souls, every one of them, in their time here on earth.

One day—with luck many, many years in the future—their secrets will die with her, a peaceful, timely, and quiet death, unlike their own.

Until then, Shea carries the wisdom and strength born of all that tragedy, and she carries the truth.

MOLLY

Molly sits cross-legged on the floor across from Dawson, stacking wooden blocks so that he can topple them with a swipe of his hand, a game that never grows old for him. Ordinarily, she'd bask in his giddy glee every time he knocks them over, but right now, she's plugged into the podcast about Chantal.

She can see why Riley Robertson is so popular. She's engaging and knowledgeable, not just reporting on a cold case but doing her best to solve it. She interviews countless people who'd worked with Chantal along with experts in everything from mental health to meteorology.

Molly listens with fascination to a segment about the weather patterns occurring the September Chantal vanished—hot, dry, and windy, with wildfires burning in the area, just like now. Riley leads the guests—a meteorologist, a psychotherapist, and a folklore expert—in a lively debate about whether the Santa Ana winds had contributed in any way to whatever had happened to Chantal.

The meteorologist cited wind speeds capable of knocking over an average-sized person.

"So if that person was too close to the edge of a precipice and a gust blew up behind her, she'd fall right over the edge," Riley said. "Think about it, listeners. Maybe it was predestined. Wind . . . fall . . . Windfall."

The psychotherapist referred to scientific studies showing that the winds create atmospheric electrification resulting in positive ionizations that can have a profound impact on mood and behavior.

The folklore expert said that some early Californians believed that the winds were laced with evil spirits, contaminating the very air people breathed so that they could become possessed.

Riley talks on and the wind blows and Molly stacks blocks and Dawson knocks them down. Her bruised head is throbbing and her thoughts are racing.

She thinks of Leila, drinking too much and saying too much last night, and now gone. And of Beck's controlling attitude, and of Shea, who'd known Chantal, and of the woman J.J. had seen outside and the one Molly had seen on the balcony.

Even J.J. is unfamiliar now, silently brooding and not wearing the glasses that have always been such a part of her. It seems silly, letting something so superficial impact how Molly perceives her friend, but it's just *off*. Everything, everyone around her, feels off, and she's trapped in this place and time where the hills are burning and the wind is toxic and women disappear.

J.J.

J.J. slips out into the hall and listens. All is still inside the house. Outside, the wind is raging. She glances at Molly's closed door at the end of the hall, then turns away.

I'll be back, she promises silently, hurrying toward the stairs.

There's no way Molly and Dawson can accompany her out of here on foot. Molly wouldn't make it to the end of the long driveway carrying the baby, let alone however far it is from here to civilization.

And that's if she even agrees to leave. More likely, she'll want J.J. to go out to the water and call the police. Or call John and tell him to send help.

I guess I'll do anything not to have to handle a problem on my own . . . Life is so much easier when you get to lean on someone.

J.J. should have pointed out how fortunate Molly is to have gotten this far always having someone to lean on. She should have said a lot of things.

But there's still time. This isn't goodbye.

I swear I'll be back, Molly.

She descends the stairs as quietly as she can, prepared for jingling dog tags and barking below. But the dogs are silent.

Shea must have driven off with them in the Porsche, leaving J.J. and Molly at the mercy of her armed henchman. Or maybe the fires are encroaching and he's with her, and they're saving themselves and leaving J.J. and Molly and Dawson to be burned alive.

Bile rushes into her throat and she yanks open the door.

Beck is there, on the other side of it, as if he'd been waiting for her. She can feel his gaze probing her, though his eyes are masked by aviator sunglasses. She swallows the bile with a lump of fear.

"Everything okay, J.J.?"

"Yes!" The reply is too quick, too shrill. "Why?"

"Just asking. You seem a little shell-shocked."

Behind him, she spots the dogs. Mel is nosing around in the gravel, and Lola is chasing something invisible along the walkway.

"I'm just . . . I was just feeling a little nauseous," J.J. tells Beck.

"Have you eaten anything today?"

"I . . . I don't think so. But I thought maybe some fresh air . . ."

"I'd say this is anything but," he comments, waving a hand at the hazy atmosphere.

Her pulse pounds. She clears her throat. "Do you know where Shea is?"

"She went out to make a call."

"To the police?"

"I don't know."

"Oh." She hesitates, the skin on the back of her neck prickling.

"Does that mean the road is open now?"

"No, it's still closed."

Don't give anything away. Just excuse yourself and get away from him.

He's squarely positioned on the doorstep, blocking her exit. Is it deliberate? What if he tries to stop her from leaving the house? And why is he wearing sunglasses when the sun is blocked by all this smoke?

"You said Shea left," she reminds him, "so I assumed the road must be open."

"I just mean she went out to the water, hoping she could get a signal."

Either he's lying, or she's paranoid.

Don't let him see that you're suspicious. Be casual.

Yeah, so much for that. She's staring so hard at the spot where the Porsche had been parked that he turns his head and follows her gaze.

"I moved her car," he comments.

"Why?"

"It was in the defensible zone."

"What . . . what do you mean?"

"It's combustible. The gas tank? I parked it away from the house. Just in case."

"In case . . . ?"

"In case the fires spread. With this wind, you just don't know."

Fire.

Wind.

The wind can shift and the next thing you know, you've lost everything.

Again, she swallows a tide of bile.

Beck reaches into his jacket pocket.

"What are you doing?" The question flies out of her with shrill urgency.

He pauses and looks at her, then pulls out . . . a protein bar.

"Here," he says. "You should eat this. You look like you're going to keel over."

J.J. exhales, allowing him to press it into her hand.

"Thank you," she murmurs, and hurries back into the house.

SHEA

Shea finds Beck out front, playing fetch with the dogs. Well, with Lola, though he's trying to coax Mel into the game.

"He wouldn't chase a stick unless it was a raw meaty bone," she informs him, and Beck turns. "Why the sunglasses?"

"It poked out a little while ago. I moved your car to a safe spot away from the house."

"Thanks. I was going to do that. I talked to Justin, and he said the fires are spreading. We need to get those two and the baby out of here." She nods at the house.

"Good idea. Is Justin sending a car for them?"

"He can't. You'll have to drive them back to LA."

"My car is a few miles down the road."

"Right. Can you please go get it and bring it up here?"

"Shea—"

"I know the roadblocks might still be up, but if you explain that you need it to evacuate two women and an infant, I'm sure they'll—"

"Shea?"

"Oh, and the dogs. You can bring them to Justin, and he'll arrange a hotel for the others."

"Shea."

"What!" she snaps.

"We'll all go."

The man is infuriatingly calm.

Struggling to keep hers, she says, "You can't possibly expect those two women to haul themselves and a baby all the way down to your car."

"No, I mean, we'll all evacuate. I'm not leaving you here alone."

"This is my home. I live here. Alone."

"And two women have vanished from this place."

"I promise you that Chantal's disappearance has nothing to do with Leila running off with a billion dollars."

"You want to tell me how you can be so sure of that?"

"No."

He sighs and takes off his sunglasses, fixing her with a narrowed gaze. "Shea? I saw someone, okay?"

"What are you talking about?"

"I was heading back toward the house from where I left the car, and I came through the trees and there was a woman with binoculars, looking at the house. She saw me and took off."

"Not Leila?"

"I didn't get a good look."

"Could it have been Leila?"

"Yes. Or Chantal." He stares into her eyes. "Shea? Do you—"

"I can't talk about this right now."

"Now? Or never?"

She shrugs, turns, and walks away.

"You *can't* talk about it?" he calls after her. "Or you *won't?*"

She ignores him, heading into the house, lugging other people's secrets like an iron chain shackling her to the past.

MOLLY

Molly sits in the rocking chair with Dawson on her lap. She's still listening to the podcast, turning the pages of a picture board book and pointing at colorful images, telling him what they are in lieu of reading the rhyming text.

"Truck, Dawson," she says.

He makes the *T* sound. "T-t-t . . ."

"No one from her past ever recognized her and came forward," Riley Robertson says in Molly's ear.

Molly turns the page. "Kitty cat. See? Meow."

Dawson babbles, "M-m-m . . ."

Molly turns the page.

"She was a true chameleon, my friends," Riley says.

"Chameleon," Molly murmurs, though she's pointing at a banana.

From Dawson: "C-c-c . . ."

"And chameleons regularly shed their skin."

Dawson makes a fussy sound, trying to turn the page.

"Oops, sorry, sweetie. You're right. Next page."

She jumps at a sharp knock on the door, so loud it's

audible above Dawson's chattering and Riley Robertson's speculating.

Molly pauses the podcast, removes her earbuds, and goes to the door, carrying Dawson and the book.

"Who's there?" she calls.

"It's me. J.J."

She opens the door, and does a double take. "You look like you've seen a ghost—again."

"Not a ghost. It's just that guy, Beck . . . he moved the car."

"What car?"

"Shea's Porsche." J.J. comes into the room. "You should lock the—"

Molly is already sliding the bolt, an expert now at locking it with one hand while holding the baby with the other.

"He moved Shea's Porsche?"

"Yes. He hid it somewhere."

"He *hid* it? He hid the car?"

"Well, he said he moved it because of the fires, but I don't trust him. About anything."

"I don't, either. J.J. . . . do you think he did something to Leila? And now he's going to do something to us?"

"I don't know. But I keep thinking . . . wouldn't he have done it already?" She rubs her temples.

"Is your head still hurting?"

"Yes. It's just stress. And eye strain, and the smoke. It's so overpowering. Isn't it bothering you?"

Molly breathes in through her nose. "All I smell is him."

She gestures at the baby. "And that wouldn't have been a good thing before I changed him, but now it is."

J.J. musters a smile.

"Since he can't break your glasses this time, do you want to hold him again? It might make you feel better."

She hesitates, then says, "Sure."

Molly hands him over. "He knows you. See? He loves his Auntie J.J. You should sit in the rocker. It's comfy."

J.J. nods and sits.

Molly gathers up the blocks scattered across the floor. "I've been listening to the podcast and thinking about Leila. And Stef."

"Oh, Molly . . ."

"No, not like that. The point is that now that I know, I can believe that she took our ticket and our money and ran away—with Stef, or someone else, or even by herself. And it should be easy enough to find out at least part of the answer."

"How?"

"Check with Stef. Go out by the water and call him." She waves her phone at J.J.

"You have his number?"

"So do you, unless he's changed it in the past twenty years."

"I'm sure he did."

"He didn't."

"If you haven't called him in years, then how do you know?"

"What I *said* was that I haven't *seen* him in years."

"But you've talked to him since college?"

"A few times." Molly busies herself arranging the blocks in a bin. "He invited us all to his wedding, remember? I couldn't go, for whatever reason. I called to tell him, and we chatted for a while, and he seemed really happy with her."

"And that's the last time you ever talked to him?"

"No, there was one other time."

"When?"

"Gosh, I don't know. Years ago. He was in Atlanta on business, and I guess he thought I lived there."

J.J. rolls her eyes. "At least he had the right state."

"I told him it was a four-hour drive. He wanted me to meet up with him anyway."

"That's so Stef. So presumptuous. Please tell me you didn't do it."

"Of course not. I told him I was in rehearsals for a play and couldn't get away."

"Not true?"

"No."

"I'm glad you knew it wouldn't be a good idea."

"Well, it's not like he said he wanted anything other than to have a few drinks and talk about old times. He was married, and all."

"Come on, Molly, who are you kidding? You knew exactly what he was looking for. Once a cad, always a cad, you know?"

She nods, returning the blocks to the shelf, aligning the bin just so with the others.

"It's good that you didn't go."

"It is. So can you go call him?"

"*Me?* Why don't you?"

Molly turns away from the toy shelf. "I can't lug the baby around looking for a signal."

"I'll stay here with him. You're right. Holding Dawson makes everything a little better." She flashes a smile.

Molly returns the smile, but it fades quickly.

"The thing is, J.J., I'm not comfortable calling Stef."

"Well, I'm not, either. What would I even say?"

"Just ask him if he knows where Leila is."

"But what do you think he's going to say? Either he's as clueless as we are, and then we have to explain, or he's with her and they're running away and he's not going to tell us that, is he?"

Molly opens a desk drawer, pulls out a small notepad and pen, and consults her phone. She scribbles Stef's number on the paper, and holds it out to J.J.

"If I'm going to call him, shouldn't I do it from your phone? He might not answer for a number he doesn't recognize."

She's right. Molly hadn't considered that.

But if she hands over her phone, J.J. will have access to everything that's on it.

She might not go snooping through it, but if she does . . .

"I'm in the middle of listening to this podcast on my

phone." She shoves Stef's number into J.J.'s hand. "It's pretty much the only thing that's keeping me sane right now. Call him from yours. I'm sure he'll pick up even if he thinks it's a telemarketer. Remember how he used to make small talk with the most random people?"

"Not really."

Watching J.J. put the paper into her pocket, Molly wants more than anything to tell her the truth—about everything.

For months now, she's been longing to unburden herself on someone who will accept that she's a liar and love her anyway. Her mother, one of her sisters, J.J. . . .

Leila is the only person she never considered telling, even though you could always count on Leila to offer sound advice.

Molly isn't seeking advice. That wouldn't change what happened or the lies she told. She'd promised herself she'd carry the secret to her grave, but what if her life really is in danger now? No one will ever know the truth.

Maybe that would be for the best. The moment she tells anyone, there will be no going back.

Dawson whines in J.J.'s arms, reaching toward Molly.

"I'll take him," she says. "He's tired. I'll put him down for a nap. You can go make that call."

Dawson whimpers in her arms.

"Everything's going to be okay," she whispers, as much to herself as to him.

Thank goodness he's too young to realize that anything

is off. All he cares about is sleeping and eating. As long as he can do those things, all is well in his world.

For now, anyway.

As she settles him into his crib, he gazes up at her with sleepy blue eyes.

"I love you," she whispers. "Even if you do look just like your daddy."

J.J.

Back in her suite, J.J. lights a cigarette.

She told Molly that if Beck had done something to Leila and intends to harm the two of them as well, he'd already have done it.

That part is true.

But she didn't share everything she was thinking. She doesn't want Molly ruminating about Leila and Stef with the possibility of hidden microphones or Beck within earshot.

Part of her believes that's sheer paranoia. Another part of her suspects that Beck—or Beck and Shea—know exactly what happened to Leila, and they're just stringing J.J. and Molly along until they can—

She cries out, spotting a strange woman standing across the room.

Realizing it's merely her own reflection in the wide wall mirror, she freezes with the cigarette poised in her hand, waiting for someone—Molly? Beck?—to bang on the door and ask what's going on.

Nobody does.

Molly is down at the other end of the hall and might not have heard anything. If Beck was lurking nearby, he would have.

Okay, so maybe she is just paranoid. Maybe things really are as they seem to be. Maybe Beck and Shea have no idea where Leila is, and J.J. and Molly are safe here for now.

The woman in the mirror doesn't seem convinced.

J.J. steps closer to examine the reflection.

No wonder she'd thought a stranger had entered the room.

She doesn't recognize herself without her glasses, as much because she's nearsighted without them as because they're such a perpetual part of her face. And this woman looks far more haggard than the woman she used to be, and the one her mind's eye still imagines she is.

You could be a knockout if you'd just put a little effort into your appearance . . .

That might have been true back when Leila said it, freshman year, but no longer.

Even now, the memory stings. They'd been in the dorm bathroom, all three of them, sharing sinks and mirrors as they got ready for class.

For Leila, that involved a curling iron and complicated cosmetic ritual. For J.J., it meant brushing her teeth *and* her hair.

She remembers looking up from the sink to find Leila scrutinizing her.

"You could be a knockout if you'd just put a little effort into your appearance."

Molly's plucked, penciled eyebrows shot up beneath a headful of hot rollers. "Geez Louise, Leila. What a thing to say!"

"J.J. knows I don't mean anything bad by it. I'm just giving honest advice. If she used some makeup and fixed her hair and—"

"Leila! Stop criticizing her!"

"It's constructive criticism! I'm just pointing that if she—"

"Leila! Stop!"

J.J. had remained silent through the exchange, studying her own reflection in the mirror just as she is now.

That day, she saw a plain Jane who might indeed benefit from a makeover. Not that she had the slightest clue how or where to begin. Anyway, she had no money or time to waste on frivolous things. Every penny she earned went to necessities, every spare minute to her campus job and academics.

"If your grades slip, you can kiss your scholarship goodbye," her mother had warned her. "And if you lose your scholarship, you'll have to get yourself back home and find a job."

Her grades hadn't slipped. She'd graduated magna cum laude.

Pursuing a masters degree in creative writing was out of the question, as was moving to New York, much less writing a novel. She had to earn a living. Literary opportunities were nonexistent in Saint Louis, so she took the first job that presented itself: in the billing department at the hospital where her mother was a receptionist.

Every day, Carolyn Johnson sat at the front desk and greeted patients and staff with a pleasant smile. Dozens of physicians walking past her without even seeing her . . .

If even one of them had bothered to look at her, really look, they might have seen the jaundice and weight loss that were so evident to J.J. when she came home from Northwestern. They might have heard the nagging cough and suspected Carolyn was sick, in the earliest stages of the cancer that would claim her life less than two years later.

J.J. had noticed and chalked it up to the usual.

Overworked and overtired; underpaid and underfed.

Leila's words, last night.

There's never enough. Not enough time, or money, or . . . me. I'm just . . . never enough.

It's the story of J.J.'s life—and her mother's death.

She walks toward the bed, so inviting with the fluffy duvet and piles of pillows.

She sits down and picks up the orange prescription bottle on the bedside table.

Anyone would be anxious in this situation, too.

Anxious? Most people would panic. She's on the verge of it.

She shakes the bottle, hoping she has enough pills to get her through to the other side of this hellish situation. The instructions are *prn*—take as needed—and she's needed more than usual lately, beginning last weekend with all the travel and stress.

The last pill she'd taken hasn't kicked in yet—or is it no longer working? What time had she'd taken it? She tries to organize her thoughts around the events of the day, but it all seems so fuzzy.

Breathe. In . . . out . . . in . . . out . . .

A panic attack can trigger your fight-or-flight instinct . . .

The perception of danger isn't grounded in reality . . .

"Yes it is," she tells Dr. Michaels's voice. "This time it is. This is dangerous."

She can't afford to spiral into a panic attack when her very life depends on staying calm, keeping her wits about her.

She swallows a pill. It might be too soon to take it, but that's better than too late.

She sinks back into the pillows and stares at the ceiling, waiting to slip away to a blissful, far-off place where none of this ever happened.

If only she were back home with John beside her. Yes, and Brian right down the hall—Dawson's age. Colicky, even.

Holding that baby, breathing his sweet scent, hadn't calmed J.J.'s anxiety, as Molly had predicted and J.J. had claimed. It had made her long for her own son, young enough to still be safely under his parents' roof.

She closes her eyes and imagines herself there.

And then, somehow, she really is back there. Back home, with John.

"I need you," she tells him, trying to get him to put his arms around her, but he keeps wrenching himself from her grasp. "Please, John! I need to know everything's going to be okay, even though—"

"He's missing! Where is he?"

In the dream—the nightmare—she realizes that Leila isn't missing. It's her son. Her baby. Brian. She and John race around the apartment, frantically searching.

"Call someone!" she screams. "Call for help!"

"You call. I'm not comfortable." John has become Molly, giving her a piece of paper with a number written on it.

J.J. tries to dial it but her phone in the shatterproof case has been shattered, and now Molly is gone and John is gone and she has to find Brian . . .

Fight or flight . . .

Fight or flight . . .

She runs outside, onto an urban street and she looks back to see not her apartment building but a Spanish mansion by the sea and it's on fire. Everything. The house, hillside, even the sea. Everything is burning, burning.

"Tell me where he is!" John screams at her.

"I don't know!" she sobs.

"You're lying!"

John, too, is on fire, flames in his hair, engulfing his clothes, obscuring his face, and he's too close to the edge, and then he's falling, falling, and she's screaming his name and the phone is shattered but it's ringing, ringing . . .

Hi, guys, welcome to *Disappearing Acts*. I'm host Riley Robertson, former investigative reporter, current podcaster, and perennial snoop!

On today's episode of *Whatever Happened to Chantal Charbonneau?*, we're going to talk about what happened in the years after her disappearance.

It took five years for her to be declared dead. She'd left her entire estate to Patrick and Josephine Daniels, the married couple who lived at Windfall and served as her groundskeeper and housekeeper. As we discussed in last week's episode about the investigation, they had been questioned and cleared of any involvement in her disappearance.

A number of people attempted to contest her will, from her longtime manager to strangers claiming to be her illegitimate offspring or distant French relatives. None were successful.

Chantal wasn't the first eccentric millionaire to leave everything to her domestic staff, and her attorney and witnesses confirmed she had been of sound mind when she named her heirs. By all accounts, Patrick and Josephine were trusted confidants and exemplary employees who were fiercely protective of Chantal and her privacy. Chantal doted on the Danielses' daughters and had set up significant trust funds for them.

Unfortunately, the Windfall Curse didn't end with Chantal's disappearance.

Six months later, the Danielses' older daughter, Corey, died of a drug overdose at sixteen. Patrick and Josephine squandered their fortune and met a bloody end, gunned down by a reputed loan shark in front of their younger daughter, Shea, who escaped unharmed.

She continues to live at Windfall, the last place Chantal was ever seen alive. Windfall is also the name of her business, a sudden-wealth consultancy committed to sparing ultrahigh net worth individuals the potentially deadly misfortunes that come with a fortune.

Shea Daniels has steadfastly maintained that she has no idea what became of Chantal Charbonneau.

Do you believe her?

I don't.

SATURDAY EVENING

MOLLY

"I don't believe Shea, either," Molly tells Riley Robertson, and presses Pause on the podcast, eyes wide.

Shea must have some idea what happened to Chantal. She'd been ten years old when the actress disappeared; had lived in this house at the time; had been one of the only people in the world to have had a close relationship with her.

What if she knows what happened to Leila, too? What if she made it happen?

Molly walks over to the crib.

She'd put Dawson down for a nap a while ago—how long ago? Half an hour? Two hours? Time has lost significance in this nightmare of a day, now giving way to dusk.

She'd never answered her mother's texts, had never made an excuse for not showing up at the barbecue today.

She imagines the whole family gathered in her parents' tiny backyard. There aren't enough seats for everyone, and the nieces and nephews are running wild while her sisters gossip and Mom worries that her brothers-in-law are burning the food on the grill and her dad keeps sneaking Dawson bites of sugary treats . . .

She feels a lump rise in her throat at the ordinariness of it all.

Who needs tens—or hundreds—of millions of dollars?

She just wants to get out of here and go home.

Guilt mingles with longing. They must be worried sick about her. They don't deserve this.

She'd made such a point to Leila about being unable to lie to her parents, yet even that had been a lie.

As Riley Robertson pointed out in an earlier episode, actresses are chameleons, skilled at shedding their skin and convincing people that they're someone else.

Molly has been doing it for months, fooling everyone, including herself.

How long can she go on seeing only what she wants to see; telling herself what she wants to hear? Is that what she'll do with her son? Hide her true self?

How long before he's old enough to see right through her? What then? Will he pity her?

Worse yet, what if he turns out the same way? Delusional about himself, dependent on other people.

She pivots away from the crib and paces to the balcony door. The sky is an otherworldly shade of red, a reminder that somewhere beyond the smoke screen the sun is setting and night is falling.

Don't ever let anything happen to your son. You have to protect him. Keep him close to you.

J.J.'s words hadn't seemed ominous twenty-four hours ago.

Now they're trapped in this cursed mansion. It's time to do take control and do something, before it's too late.

SHEA

Twice this afternoon, Shea had made the long walk out to the sea only to find that there was no phone signal.

Now it's dusk, and the third time is a charm.

Justin answers the call as if he was holding the phone and waiting to hear from her, which is probably the case.

"You're alive!" he exclaims, so loudly that she winces and holds the phone away from her ear, switching it to speakerphone.

"Did you think otherwise?"

"I was starting to wonder."

"I just couldn't get service until now." She shifts her gaze from the sea to the eastern hillside beyond the house, still shrouded in smoke and now in encroaching darkness. "Any update on the fires?"

"They've contained the one just east of you, but a new one's flared up to the north."

"Terrific."

Earlier, Beck had left the house and walked down the road to see if it was open yet and get his car back up to the house. He returned on foot, saying there are still barricades and they're still working on repairs to the communications grid.

"Has Leila turned up yet?" Justin asks her.

"No. Did you get any information?"

"Yes. There's a lot. I don't even know where to start."

"Start with her family. Are the daughters and boyfriend accounted for?"

"Yes. I found his teaching schedule online and I know he's there today because one of his students is posting snarky comments about his outfit in real time, from the classroom, with photos."

"His *outfit*?"

"He's wearing cargo pants with a tie. And Crocs."

"Maybe he likes pockets. And comfort. And this isn't *Project Runway*. What about the daughters?"

"I drove over to her condo. Nobody's home, but the next-door neighbor turned out to be a wonderful busybody. She told me that Leila and her ex-husband share custody and that they had a big fight on the phone about him keeping the girls this weekend."

"Leila told her that?"

"No, she overheard the whole thing. She said the walls are thin, but she seems like the type who'd be leaning against one with a glass to her ear."

"So she might have heard Leila talking about the lottery win."

And maybe she's not the only one. What if the wrong person overheard something and had the right connections?

Shea's mind whirls with possibilities as Justin talks on.

"The ex-husband's name is Warren McGovern and he lives in Anaheim. I called to confirm that the girls are with him."

"What did you tell him?"

"That I'm a colleague of Leila's and I was trying to reach her and—"

Shea waits. After a moment she says, "And what? Justin? Justin?"

The call has dropped. She sees that there's no service.

She paces, wondering how long it will be before Beck notices that she slipped out of the house again. He'd told her—twice—that he wanted to accompany her.

"You shouldn't go alone after dark, Shea. You might get into trouble out there."

"Then I'll get myself out."

"Yeah, you're pretty experienced at that, aren't you?"

"What?"

"You're pretty experienced at getting yourself out of things."

"What's that supposed to mean?"

"Never mind. I just think you should be listening to me. You're not used to dealing with this kind of thing. I am."

"You're used to dealing with missing lottery winners?"

"You know what I mean."

She does, and is even more determined to handle this on her own. That's how it works after a breakup. You're on your own. You don't get to rely on the other person for anything, ever again.

You're pretty experienced at getting yourself out of—

Her phone rings and she jumps. Justin again.

"Still alive," she says, putting the call on speaker. "Keep talking. Fast, in case I lose you again. You confirmed the girls are with their father."

"Yes. And I found Stef Kiley. He lives in Escondido, just north of San Diego. Married with four kids and a couple of dogs and cats. He posts on social media almost as often as your pal Cyphyr does—pictures of the kids, the wife, the pets, the house, the food, and a lot of selfies. His last post was a video of his daughter's ballet recital Thursday night, and let me tell you, the kid is no Misty Copeland."

"Okay, Justin? This isn't *Dancing with the Stars*, either. Get back to Leila. Could she have run off with Stef?"

"I don't know about that, but remember how you asked me to look into the others? Molly, J.J., Leila's family, the neighbors. . . ."

"Yes?"

"Yeah, well . . . you're not going to believe what I just found."

"Shea?" another voice says, not on the phone, but behind her, and she turns to see Beck.

She opens her mouth, but before she can protest his presence, Justin goes on talking, and she knows it isn't an earthquake, but the ground seems to shake and tilt beneath her feet.

J.J.

Beneath a strange orange sky, J.J. finds her way back to the shed, armed with a flashlight she'd found in the mudroom and a kitchen knife she'd grabbed on her way out the door, just in case.

Heart pounding, she stands for a long time on the stone slab that serves as a doorstep, waiting for the latest dose of medication to kick in, and listening. For what, she isn't sure. Footsteps? Voices?

She hears nothing but wind and water and her own ragged breathing and then the creak of the door when she pushes it open, and the click of the flashlight's button as she illuminates the space within.

All the outdoor furniture is neatly stacked, including the chair and table that had been separated earlier. The phone cord and protein bar wrapper and empty soda can—ashtray are gone.

She steps in and takes a closer look, because she doesn't have her glasses and it's all blurry. But she isn't blind.

She thrusts a long, trembling breath from her body as

if making room for the thing that's been trying to force its way past the haze in her brain.

"No," she says aloud, shaking her head. "You didn't imagine it. You aren't crazy."

She turns and walks away, back to the house, silently repeating it like a mantra.

You aren't crazy.

You aren't crazy.

Noxious smoke stings her eyes, and then tears do. She shoves a hand into her pocket, looking for a tissue and finding the knife's sharp blade. It slices into the tender flesh of her thumb—not deep, but there's blood.

And it isn't her thumb but her mother's: not her blood but her mother's.

They're back in J.J.'s kitchen, back twenty years, to the December when J.J. was enormously pregnant and her mother was still alive and illness had forced her to move into the spare room her daughter and son-in-law had intended as a nursery.

That night—the last night—she'd been trying to help J.J. make dinner because they had to eat. There was no money for takeout with Carolyn's medical bills added to the household budget, even with J.J. working right up to her due date and John taking double shifts.

"Sit down. You shouldn't be on your feet after such a long day," her mother said.

"Neither should you, Mom. You sit down."

But Carolyn insisted on chopping the onions for whatever J.J. was cobbling together.

She cut her thumb.

It bled more than it should have. Her mother nearly fainted.

J.J. brought her to the hospital. They admitted her overnight as a precaution.

The phone rang in the middle of the night. When J.J. answered it, an unfamiliar woman's voice identified itself as the attending physician and informed her that her mother was gone.

"Gone?" J.J. echoed, misunderstanding. "Where could she go? She lives with me, and I dropped her off. Maybe she just went looking for coffee, or—"

"What I mean is that she passed away," the doctor said. "I'm so sorry."

"From a cut on her thumb? You must have the wrong patient."

But the doctor had the right patient. She explained that the cancer battle had depleted Carolyn's body and she wasn't able to fight off what could have been a minor infection.

Two weeks later, Brian was born. Three weeks after that, J.J.'s obstetrician referred her to a psychiatrist for postpartum depression.

Even now, J.J. isn't convinced of Dr. Michaels's diagnosis. Yes, she'd been depressed, and yes, she'd recently given birth. But she'd also recently lost her mother, and she rarely saw her husband, who was working around the clock to cover the extra bills, leaving J.J. alone in the bleak apartment with a colicky newborn.

Anyone would have been depressed. It didn't mean she had some kind of . . . condition.

Dr. Michaels gave her medication. It helped numb the pain. Eventually, she got better.

Anyone would have, with time. Her grief ebbed and the baby grew out of colic and the dreary winter weather gave way to spring. It didn't mean the medication was working.

That's what she told herself, and John, back then.

It's what she tells herself now as she sucks blood from her thumb and fumbles in her other pocket.

No tissue.

But there is something . . .

She pulls out a crumpled protein bar wrapper.

You aren't crazy.

You aren't crazy.

You aren't—

"J.J.!"

She looks up.

Molly is on the balcony.

"Come up here," she calls in a hushed voice. "Please? I need you."

SHEA

Shea hangs up the phone and stares at Beck, wide-eyed.

"Did you—"

"Yes. I heard."

"Do you think it's true?"

"He said he'd text you a link so you can see for yourself."

She nods and looks down at her phone. Nothing yet.

"Where are they?" she asks Beck, not looking up. "Molly and the baby? J.J.?"

"In their rooms. Everything seems okay for now."

"*Seems* isn't very reassuring, is it? Neither is *for now*. Shouldn't you be back there, keeping an eye on things? Did you have to come hiking all the way out here because you don't think I'm capable of—"

"Believe me, I know you're the most capable woman in the world."

That catches her by surprise.

Even more so than *You're pretty experienced at getting yourself out of things.*

He'd been referring to their relationship. Last December, she'd flown to South America to spend two weeks with him before he started a new assignment.

They spent their days lazing around the villa, nights in each other's arms, and dawns jogging on the beach as the sun's first rays glistened on the horizon and soared to ignite the world in their warm glow.

During that final sunrise on a deserted beach, she'd finally said the words she'd gone there to say in the first place.

"We can't keep doing this."

There was a long pause. He never broke his barefoot pace along the wet sand. She didn't look at him, aware that she wouldn't have seen anything other than sunglasses and his poker face anyway.

"Why?" he asked, eventually.

"Things aren't working out for us."

"You mean things aren't working out for you."

"Things aren't working out for me, and I think you'd say the same about you."

"Don't put words into my mouth."

"Fair enough. Things aren't working out for me."

"So you haven't had an amazing couple of weeks here with me?"

"No, I did! It's been amazing, but . . . this isn't real life. There's no place for you—for this, for us—in my real life."

They fell silent, and she reminded herself of all the reasons they couldn't be together.

Nine months later, she can't remember a damned one.

Now here he is, standing in front of her, his face cloaked in shadows and fire just as it had been that last morning.

"If you think I'm so capable," she says, "then why did you follow me out here?"

"Because a sheriff's deputy buzzed the gate with an evacuation advisory. It means—"

"I know what it means." The threat isn't imminent—yet. But it's coming.

Her phone buzzes in her hand.

She looks down to see the text from Justin, and her eyes widen.

MOLLY

Molly senses J.J.'s weariness—and wariness—as she climbs the steps from the courtyard to the balcony.

"What's wrong?"

"Just come inside. And shh, Dawson is asleep."

She locks the balcony door after J.J. and turns to see that she's sucking her thumb and her eyes are wide and a little wild. It's as if she's been transformed into a terrified child.

"J.J., what—"

Then she removes her thumb from her mouth and Molly realizes that it's bleeding.

"What happened?"

"I cut myself—the gate latch has a sharp edge."

"Sit down."

Molly hurries to the bathroom, grabs a washcloth, wets it, and brings it to her friend. Somewhere in the back of her mind, her old self acknowledges that it's white and expensive and will be stained with blood.

"Is your phone still working out by the water? Did you get ahold of Stef? And John?"

"Not Stef," she says. "I talked to John."

"You told him what's been going on? What did he say?"

J.J. doesn't look at her, focused on wrapping her bloody thumb in the washcloth. "He thinks she took off. We're never going to see her again, or the money."

Molly's jaw clenches. "I think we need to call the police. If Leila took off with the ticket, it's theft. And if she didn't, something terrible happened to her."

"John said they won't even take us seriously. She's only been gone a few hours."

"She's not supposed to be gone at all! Have you listened to the podcast yet?"

"What?"

"The podcast. The one Leila told us to—"

"Oh. No."

"Well, I did, and I found out that this house is cursed."

"Because of Chantal?"

"It wasn't just her. It's Shea—her whole family. Her sister overdosed, and her parents were murdered, and now Leila—we have to get out of here, J.J."

"Molly, slow down! Murdered? Cursed? I don't know what you're talking about."

"It's all in the podcast. I can't believe Leila knew about all of this and she made us come here."

"You can't believe everything you hear on a podcast."

How can J.J. be so damned matter-of-fact? She's always

been unflappable, undramatic, unemotional, un-everything that Molly is. Yet even the most pragmatic person in the world should grasp the magnitude of this loss.

Maybe she's in denial. Or shock. Molly tries again.

"It wasn't only money, J.J. It was going to change everything. Now it's gone. Nothing's going to change for us. Our lives are just going to be—"

Her voice breaks.

"Come on, Molly. Your life is pretty damned good just as it is. You have your health. You have your son, your parents, your sisters, their families, all living right nearby . . ."

"I know." Tears stream down her face. "I know, and it should be enough, but—"

"Don't you dare say that it isn't! Don't you dare tell me that money matters more than being surrounded by all those people who love you!"

"I didn't say that!"

"You were going to."

"It doesn't matter *more*, okay? But you can't act as if it doesn't matter at all! And what about Leila? If she did this to us, then she might as well be dead."

J.J. winces. "Molly, you can't—"

"I *can*, because it's true. She's dead to us now. We lost our best friend. We lost so much, J.J." She's full-on sobbing now.

"We'll get past it." J.J. wraps her in a fierce embrace. "Come on. We're strong."

"I know, it's just . . . How am I supposed to support my son?"

"You were supporting him before. Isn't his dad paying child support?"

"No." She pulls back and looks up at J.J. "He isn't."

"*What?* How can he not pay? Is it because he's an attorney? Did he finagle some obscure loophole to get himself off the hook?"

"Ross is paying, but it's wrong. I can't let him keep doing this, because . . ." Molly takes a deep breath. "Ross isn't Dawson's father. Stef is."

J.J.

"What?" J.J. asks, though she heard it loud and clear. Her brain just can't seem to absorb the words.

Molly clears her throat. "I said—"

"No, I know what you said, but it doesn't make sense. How can Stef be Dawson's father? You said you haven't seen him in years."

"I haven't. Two years. Well, not quite two. Nineteen months."

J.J. stares at her. Dawson is ten months old. It's simple math even she can do, even in this shell-shocked state, but . . .

"No, Molly. That can't be right."

"It is."

"No. You said he came to Atlanta on business, and that he wanted to meet up, and you told him you couldn't because he was four hours away and you were rehearsing a play."

"Wow, you sure were paying attention to the details," Molly says with a nervous laugh.

"It's what you *said*! Isn't it true?"

"It is—except the part where I told Stef that I couldn't see him."

"But . . . you told me you knew it would be a bad idea, and you didn't want to dredge it all up again."

"That's true, too. It just . . . it doesn't mean I didn't do it anyway."

"So . . ." J.J. takes a deep breath. "What happened?"

"I think that part's pretty clear. Nine months later, I had Dawson."

"Why would you sleep with him? After the way he hurt you."

"That was years ago. We were kids."

"But you were married. So was he."

Molly nods. "I guess . . . I don't know why. One thing led to another, and—"

"That's such a cliché! 'One thing led to another . . .' Such a damned cliché!"

"But clichés are true. Here's another one: I regretted it immediately afterward."

"Terrific. That's awesome."

"Please don't judge me. You don't know how cold my marriage had become."

"Then why stay? Why not leave? Why cheat?"

"I don't know."

"Sure you do. Ross is rich. You stayed with him because he's rich."

Molly just stares at her, eyebrows raised.

She's so damned pretty, even now, with uncombed hair

and extra weight and raccoon mascara blending with the dark circles under her eyes. Once a beauty queen, always a beauty queen.

"It wasn't only because he was rich, J.J. It was because it's easier than being alone."

Caught off guard by her honesty, J.J. says, "Yeah, well . . . you never could stand to be alone. Or take care of yourself," she adds, twisting the knife.

She sees the wounded expression bleeding into Molly's blue eyes, yet she keeps right on stabbing at her with words she knows will hurt.

"Even back then, Molly—back in school. You went from one boyfriend to another. There was always someone hanging around to drive you somewhere or take you to dinner. The smartest ones even helped you pass calc and wrote your papers for you."

"That was a long time ago. Why are you even bringing it up?"

"Because it's still relevant. You said you were so heartbroken when Stef cheated on you! You said he was the love of your life. But you got right back out there again, didn't you?"

"Yes, and believe me, you're not telling me anything I don't already know. I just can't believe you, of all people, are talking to me this way, J.J. Why are you so angry about something that has nothing to do with you?"

"Because it does, Molly! Okay? It does have something to do with me!"

"How?"

J.J. falters. She shakes her head, tight-lipped, and looks away.

Her gaze falls on a painting above the fireplace—the figure of a woman at the edge of a seaside precipice.

"J.J.?"

She flicks her gaze back to her friend. The one and only friend she has left in the world.

And you don't know her at all. Not if this happened, and she never told you, and you never suspected it.

"You lied to me. All that stuff about how Ross won't be a part of his son's life, and how he turned his back on the baby and abandoned you to be a single mother, and how hard it is—"

"None of that is a lie."

"How can you blame Ross for turning his back on another man's son or a wife who had an affair?"

"Because he doesn't know!"

"So you lied to him, too," J.J. says, her entire body clenched. "Clearly, you often lie to people you claim to love."

"I never *lied* to Ross, and I don't even—"

"But you let him think Dawson is his!"

"Yes! When I got pregnant, I thought he might be. He could have been."

"But he isn't."

She looks down, shaking her head. "I knew the moment he was born. When I saw those blue eyes . . ."

"All babies have blue eyes. And yours are blue, too," J.J. says, as if she's trying to convince Molly that she's made a mistake.

"Not like this. And it's not just his eyes. It's everything about him. The shape of his face, and the way he smiles, and his dimple . . ."

She's right.

J.J. closes her eyes and pictures Dawson. Yeah. That little boy looks so much like Stef, she can't believe she didn't notice it right away.

"Look, J.J., I'm sorry. I'm so sorry. And I hope we can talk this all out and put it behind us, but right now . . . I just need you to do something for me, and I know I don't deserve anything, but you're the only one I can ask."

"What is it?"

"Can you just stay here with Dawson for a few minutes? I can't leave him alone here and I need to call my mother. Please, J.J.?"

Her heart is racing. She unrolls the washcloth to inspect her thumb. For the moment, the bleeding has stopped.

She looks at Molly, long and hard, and then, mind made up, says, "Sure. Go ahead. I'll stay with Dawson."

"Thank you, J.J. You're the best friend ever."

She tries to reply, clearing her throat to dislodge the lump as Molly heads for the door.

Thrusting her hand into her pocket, J.J. hurries after her, finding her voice. "Wait, Molly? One last thing . . ."

SHEA

Shea clicks the link Justin texted, with Beck leaning over her shoulder to see. They skim the page in silence. She enlarges a photo.

"That's her, right?"

"That's her," Beck confirms.

She shakes her head in disbelief, pockets her phone, and starts walking. "Let's go. We need to figure out what's going on."

We. Not *I.*

She isn't incapable, or cowardly, but this is one thing she'd prefer not to handle alone. Not knowing what she now knows. Not when it's all escalated into something far more complicated and perhaps more dangerous than she'd imagined.

Things—life, relationships—have a way of doing that.

"We need to pack up and leave, Shea," Beck tells her. "You understand that, right? All of us. Including you. I know it's your home, and I know what it means to you, but . . . it's time."

He leaves the rest unsaid.

Time to go.

Time to let go.

"How did you get into this business?" he'd asked her, not long after they met.

"I've seen how money can destroy lives. I want to save people from that."

"Because you couldn't save your family."

It wasn't a question. Of course he knew about her past, though she'd never told him. In his line of work, you don't take a job without vetting the employer as thoroughly as the employer is vetting you.

So, yes. He'd been aware before they met that her sister had been an addict, her father a gambler and heavy drinker, and her mother a frivolous, reckless spender. He knew that Corey had overdosed; that her parents' financial missteps had depleted their inheritance from Chantal and led to their murders. He knew that by the time Shea was sixteen, her family was gone, and the money was gone, except the trust fund waiting for her twenty-first birthday.

For a long time, Windfall and the memories were all she had.

And then, for a while, she had Beck.

"Do you want more?" he'd asked, that last morning on the beach when she ended things. "Is that it?"

"No, Beck. I want less."

He'd nodded and walked away without another word. Her last glimpse had been of his back, silhouetted against the rising sun as he walked away from her. He never turned for one last look. That isn't his style.

She respected him fiercely for that. Still does. It isn't her style, either.

Nor are tears, but she remembers wiping them away as she headed back along the water's edge to the empty villa. Remembers seeing the sunlight shimmering on the last traces of their footprints dissolving in the incoming tide. Remembers wondering whether she'd made the right call.

But it can't be any other way. You can't get close to someone or build a meaningful relationship without telling your secrets and letting them know who you really are.

For her, that's impossible.

The secrets she keeps aren't hers to tell, and even she doesn't know who Shea Daniels really is.

MOLLY

Clutching her phone and the flashlight J.J. had given her, Molly looks over her shoulder as she descends the balcony steps. J.J. is still there, watching from behind the French door she'd locked after Molly.

They'll be safe there, Molly assures herself, hurrying across the courtyard. She won't be gone long.

She lifts the latch and opens the gate carefully, mindful of the sharp edge, but it feels smooth beneath her fingertips.

She thinks of J.J.'s bloody thumb, of the bloodstains on the white washcloth. She forces herself to keep going, into the fiery night with the bloodred sky.

She thinks of another night, nineteen months ago, when she'd met Stef at the bar in his Atlanta hotel, a dimly lit, upscale spot with flickering votives and cozy tables. He showed her photos of his wife and kids, their luxurious home, their fabulous vacations . . .

"Wow," Molly said, two glasses of wine into the evening. "You've got the perfect life."

"Not perfect, but pretty damned great."

He told her about a recent job offer he'd turned down—a promotion, with more money, but it was based in New York. He said that there wasn't enough money in the world to get him to uproot his family, and anyway, his wife's career made them a very nice living.

"How about you, Molly? Tell me about your theater work, and your husband, and—any children?"

"Just my stepdaughters," she said, as though she'd met them more than exactly once—when she and Ross first started dating, and he thought it would be a good idea.

They'd made it clear that Molly wasn't welcome in their world, and that was fine with her. The last thing she wanted was to share her then-precious time with Ross with two en-titled young women.

"And your husband is a lawyer?" Stef asked.

"Yes. He . . . travels a lot."

"It's hard, being on the road," Stef said. "Believe me, I know. Where is he tonight?"

"He's home."

Of course Stef thought that meant Savannah, not right nearby in Buckhead. He had no idea Molly and Ross lived separate lives in separate places; no idea that Molly had been keeping an eye out for Ross all night, just in case . . .

"What does he think about your meeting up with an old boyfriend?"

"He thinks it's great."

"He must be a confident man."

"He is. What does your wife think?"

"She doesn't know, but I'm sure she'd think it was great, too."

He'd changed the subject then, talking instead about the old days.

When she caught him holding up two fingers and nodding at the bartender, she shook her head. "No more wine for me. I've got a long drive back to Savannah."

"You can always stay here."

"*What?* I can't—"

"Why not? There are plenty of rooms available. Book one and stop worrying about driving back. I'm sure your husband would be relieved."

She felt her face grow hot. She'd thought he meant for her to stay in his room. But of course he hadn't. He just wanted to catch up with an old friend.

She'd gone through the motions of excusing herself to call Ross.

"What'd he say?" Stef asked when she returned, already on his third Scotch, with another glass of wine waiting for her.

"He said to stay."

She went to the desk and booked a room.

She never set foot in it. Nor did she remember, until it was too late, that she'd gone off the pill the month before.

The next morning, waking in his rumpled king-sized bed, she heard him whistling in the shower. He'd have left her with a breezy kiss goodbye before he left for his meeting, but she said, "That's it? Aren't we going to talk about what happened?"

"What is there to say, Molly? That I'm sorry? Because I'm not. That was amazing. I'd do it again in a heartbeat."

"And you've done it before," she guessed. "With other women who aren't your wife?"

He didn't lie, or claim that his marriage was on the rocks, or that they had an agreement. He owned it completely, and he reiterated that he would never, ever leave his family. They were everything to him.

"But if you want to get together again the next time I'm in town . . ."

"No, thanks. This may be you, but it's not me."

Guilt accompanied her on the way home, so intense that she wondered whether to cancel Ross's upcoming weekend visit to Savannah. If he came, he might somehow suspect that she'd been unfaithful. Yet if he didn't come, and she found herself pregnant, there wouldn't be a hope of convincing him the baby was his.

Maybe her subconscious mind already knew, even then. Maybe she'd gone off the pill because she wanted a child. If Stef hadn't popped up when he had, the baby might have been Ross's, or perhaps some other man who walked into her life when the timing was right.

It doesn't matter. Dawson doesn't need a father in his life because he has Molly, no matter what happens with Leila and the lottery ticket. She can find a job, a real job, and earn a living on her own, and come clean with Ross and stop taking his money. She's tired, so damned tired of the lies.

Her own, and the others' . . .

Yet every time she imagines Leila making a conscious decision to steal that much money from her two best friends and run away—possibly, probably, with Stef—her brain skids to a halt.

Despite everything, Molly just can't accept that she'd do that. People change over the years, there are fundamental things you just know about someone you once knew so well, and lived with, and loved. Still love.

But if Leila hadn't stolen the money and run off, where is she? And what about one nagging fact Molly can't overlook?

She'd definitely seen someone slip from Chantal's room to the balcony earlier, and so had the dogs in the courtyard. Then J.J. had seen a woman creeping around the property. A woman who hides, and runs away. A woman who—

A figure steps out on the path in front of her, and she screams.

It's Beck.

J.J.

J.J. paces, craving a cigarette. She can't smoke one in Molly's room, though, or around the baby. Anyway, she's down to just a few left in the pack. She should probably ration them. It's going to be a long night.

A cigarette would stave off the hunger pains. She can't remember whether she's eaten anything today. A protein bar, maybe?

But not in the shed. She hadn't eaten a protein bar in the shed and drunk a can of soda and used it as an ashtray and forgotten about it.

Her heart pounds, and she can feel a panic attack coming on. She can't let that happen.

She goes to the crib and stares at Dawson, sound asleep. So sweet, so innocent . . .

Is she really going to let Molly get away with this? It's bad enough that her ex-husband is a despicable human being, according to Molly herself. But to allow Dawson to believe he's the father, and deny him the truth . . .

"No," J.J. says, struck by the unfairness of it all.

The baby startles.

His eyes open, those big blue eyes so like his daddy's. They fill with tears, and his chin quivers, and he wails.

"Oh, sweetie, it's okay. Shh, don't cry, okay? Don't cry."

She picks him up and he stiffens.

"No, shh, shh, it's okay. It's Auntie J.J. I've got you. I've got you, see?"

She gently dabs away the tears with the bloodstained washcloth, then puts him to the changing table, talking to him calmly and softly as she changes his diaper. Gradually, he stops crying.

"Are you hungry?" she asks, snapping his onesie. "I'll bet you are."

She starts to strap him into the high chair, then changes her mind and puts him into his carrier seat instead.

"B-b-b!" he says.

"Aw, are you trying to say bye-bye? Yes! We're going to go bye-bye pretty soon! You and me and your mommy!"

But what about your daddy?

He doesn't know you exist.

That isn't fair, is it? It's so unfair. But don't you worry. Auntie J.J.'s going to fix things.

"B-b-b!" he says.

"Maybe you're trying to say bottle," she says, opening the minifridge.

It's stocked with baby bottles full of milk. Or maybe it's formula. How is it that she can't remember what Brian had at this age? Her own son, her own baby. . . .

Her memory used to be so sharp. Now it's clouded with medication and fear and smoke and unsettling thoughts.

She can't let them in. She has to stay calm, for Dawson's sake. Dawson needs her. She can help him.

She shakes the bottle and removes the cap covering the rubber nipple. "Here you go, sweetie. We're going to go on a little adventure while you drink this. Just you and me."

She puts the bottle into his little hands, picks up the carrier, opens the balcony door, and slips out into the night.

MOLLY

"No!" Molly shouts as Beck grabs her shoulders. "Get away from me!"

Shea is there, too. "Molly, it's okay! It's just us!"

As if that can possibly reassure her. She wriggles beneath Beck's grip and looks from him to Shea, wild-eyed.

"Don't hurt me!"

"We're not here to hurt you," Beck says. "We're trying to help you. Why are you out here?"

"I'm going to make a phone call."

"Where?"

"By the water. There's a signal out there."

"You're heading in the opposite direction," Shea says. "The water's that way."

It's a trap. She's lying. Along with the flashlight, J.J. had given Molly careful instructions to a shortcut that would take her to the promontory.

"Molly? Where's the baby?" Beck asks.

"In the house."

"Alone?"

"J.J. has him. They're in my room. I was just . . . Look, I really need to call my mother. I'm supposed to be there, at a barbecue, and I never told her I wasn't coming." Her voice breaks. So much for the invincible attitude she'd planned to convey.

"Molly—" Shea puts a hand on her arm.

She shakes it off.

"I have to call my mother. She'll have been texting me—we text every day—and probably trying to call, too, and she'll be beside herself."

"But you shouldn't be out here in the dark alone," Beck says.

Molly lifts her chin. The last thing she needs right now—the last thing she, or any woman needs, ever—is some man telling her what she can't do.

She sees the warning look Shea sends him, as if she knows he said exactly the wrong thing.

"Molly," Shea says. "It's not that we don't think you're . . . *capable*. It's just—"

"Oh, I'm capable, and I'm doing it."

"But you're going in the wrong direction. What are you really trying to do?" Beck asks.

"I told you, I need to let my mother know that Dawson and I are okay!"

And she needs to call the police, and call someone to come get them out of this cursed place.

"First, why don't we go back and check on J.J. and the baby, okay?" Beck suggests, in a tone that stops her cold.

She takes a step back, eyes narrowing, heart pounding.

"What's going on? If you two have done anything to my baby—"

"What? No, Molly. We would never—" Shea begins, but Beck cuts her off.

"Look, there's no time to waste. There's an evacuation advisory. We need to get out of here."

"I don't believe you. You're just trying to—"

Shea cuts in this time. "Molly. This is serious."

"Why would I trust you? My friend disappeared, and you refused to call the police when J.J. and I wanted to—"

"J.J. didn't want to call the police," Beck reminds her. "Why do you think that is?"

"Because it's too soon. That's what John told her. He said they wouldn't take us seriously. He said . . ." Catching another look that passes between Shea and Beck, Molly swallows a lump of fear. "What is going on? Please?"

Beck nods at Shea.

She clears her throat. "Molly, how much do you know about the last nine months of J.J.'s life?"

J.J.

From the balcony, J.J. had watched Molly retreat into the smoky shadows, heading away from the water.

Yes, she'd felt a bit guilty sending her in the wrong direction, but she'd had no choice. She, too, has a phone call to make. Molly herself had suggested it.

I'm not comfortable calling Stef, she'd said, handing J.J. the phone number.

J.J. had tried to wiggle out of it. But now that she knows the whole story . . .

Now it's not fight or flight. It's both.

"I have to tell him," she tells Dawson as she lugs the heavy carrier up the steep path to the promontory, using her phone as a flashlight because she'd given hers to Molly.

Because she's a good friend, as Molly herself had said.

Until college, J.J. had had classmates and acquaintances but never actual friends, too shy and too focused on academics to venture into a social life. She only had her mother, and even during the years J.J. had lived at home, her mother inhabited a different world, beyond a chasm that encompassed far more than physical distance.

But Molly and Leila and Stef and a couple of others who shared a dorm corridor had been friends who were like family; more important than and closer than family, as far as J.J. was concerned.

Now Leila is gone and Molly's a liar and Stef . . .

Stef deserves the truth, just as J.J.'s father had.

Dawson deserves the truth, just as J.J. had.

Fight and flight.

She'll call Stef and she'll tell him, and she'll ask him to come here and get them. San Diego can't be that far away, and even if the road is closed, Stef has a boat.

One day, his son will tell the story of how his daddy rescued him and Auntie J.J. from the fires.

They've almost reached the promontory.

She pauses for a moment to catch her breath and check her phone. There's a signal.

She sets Dawson's carrier on the ground at her feet, fishes the phone number from her pocket, and dials.

It rings, and then he answers.

"Hello?"

J.J.'s heart leaps into her throat. Stef sounds the same as he had all those years ago, and she's catapulted back to those golden years when all had—almost—been right in the world.

"Hello?" Stef's voice says.

J.J. looks down at Molly's son, *his* son, strapped into the seat. The last time she'd checked, he'd been contentedly sucking on his bottle. Now the bottle is gone and he's start-ing to whimper and fuss.

"Hello?"

The light is different here. Night has fallen, and the sky is black, with glittering stars and a moon that lights the landscape like a stadium. Even the wind has suddenly stopped, and everything is hushed.

In the distance, alongside the platform that sits on the highest point above the ocean, she sees a woman's silhou-ette.

"Who's there?" Stef's voice asks.

Who's there . . .

Chantal Charbonneau?

Chantal's ghost?

Peering into the night, J.J. gasps. There's no mistaking the figure.

It's Leila.

MOLLY

Smoke fills Molly's lungs and fear screeches into her brain as she takes the steps to the balcony two at a time.

The door to her room is ajar.

"Dawson? Dawson!"

Beck comes up behind her as she bursts into the room. She can see at a glance that it's empty. The crib is empty.

She whirls, around and around, searching. Someone grabs her in strong, steadying arms and tells her that it's okay. They're going to find her baby.

It isn't J.J., but Shea. Shea is the one she's supposed to trust now, and J.J. is . . .

"What's wrong with her?" she wails. "Why would she do this? Why would she take my baby?"

"Try to stay calm, Molly," Beck says.

She shoves past him, opening the door to the hall, running toward J.J.'s room. They must be there. Of course they are. Because J.J. is her friend, and she would never hurt Molly, just as Leila is her friend and she would never—

She throws open the door. The room is dark and empty. She feels for a light switch on the wall and flips it.

The first thing she sees is a cluster of prescription bottles on the bedside table.

Beck and Shea are right behind her. He strides over to the table and picks up a bottle, and shakes it.

"Empty," he says, and picks up another one. "This is, too."

"She said she needed something to help her sleep," Molly murmurs, remembering. "Last night. And Leila told her not to worry about mixing the medication with alcohol."

Shea is checking labels. "There's a lot more here than just sleeping pills. She's on some powerful psych meds. And these prescriptions were all filled a little over a week ago. They shouldn't be empty already, and she shouldn't be mixing any of this with alcohol or with anything else."

"She has Dawson," Molly says. "We have to find them. The fires . . . we have to find them and get out of here!"

"We'll search the house, and the property," Beck says. "They couldn't have gotten far."

J.J.

"Leila!" J.J. screams, standing high above the crashing sea, but the word is lost in the waves and wind. "Leila!"

Relief had surged through her when she'd spotted her friend. If Leila is out there, alive and well, then J.J. must have hallucinated the terrible thing that had happened before.

It's rare, but it can happen, Dr. Michaels had told her at a recent session, right after she'd awakened in the night to find John standing over the bed.

He wasn't really there.

But Leila had been. J.J. is certain of that. She'd stood in the window and the sky had been clear and the moon had been bright and there was no mistaking Leila, on the cliff.

Now she's gone, and the moon is gone, and the night sky is low above the water, thick with . . .

It isn't mist. It's smoke. No wonder her heart is racing, and she feels as though she can't catch her breath. She has to find Leila and they have to get out of here away from this terrible, cursed place.

"Leila! Where are you?"

J.J. feels dizzy, standing out in the smoky open air so high above sea, scanning for Leila's head bobbing in the waves, or flailing arms, an outstretched hand.

"Leila!"

Then she hears it.

A baby's cry, loud and shrill above the ocean's roar, close . . . so close . . .

She looks down, dumbfounded to find that she's holding a baby carrier. There's a little boy in it.

"Brian! Oh, thank goodness! I thought . . . I thought . . ."

She shakes her head, feeling as though the smoke is clouding her brain, shrouding reality. Somehow, she'd thought her son had grown up and become a Marine and left her, just as everyone else had done, but he's right here.

That was just another hallucination.

"J.J.!"

Another sound, off in the distance.

She turns, slowly.

Three figures are coming toward her.

The first is a man.

Not John.

Because John . . .

John is . . .

SHEA

The last traces of red tint the night sky and the wind blows clouds of smoke as Shea makes her way along the path that leads out past the tennis courts and pool and storage shed. She trains the flashlight beam to the left and right, keeping an eye out for any sign of J.J. and the baby.

In the distance, she can hear Beck and Molly calling to each other. They'd split up, the three of them, to search the property. There's a lot of ground to cover, and no telling where J.J. might be, and what she might do.

Shea had been stunned when Justin revealed that her husband, John, had died nine months ago.

"But she's been talking about him, and calling him . . . are you sure?"

"I'm positive. I'll send you the link to the obituary and press coverage of the funeral. She's in the photos."

She was, above a caption that identified her as the widow.

Seeing her stricken expression and stiff posture, Shea's heart ached for her. She understands crippling grief; knows that it can break you, destroy your relationships, rob you of your sanity and your will to live.

Shea had fled the house on the day her sister died.

She remembers a bird, a beautiful dove, soaring just beyond her grasp. In her memory, it was Corey, beckoning her. In reality, it was probably a dirty seagull—flying rats, her mother called them.

She remembers the splintery feel of the wooden railing beneath her leg, bare in her private school uniform skirt. She remembers her father's voice shouting her name, and how he'd grabbed her arm, dislocating her shoulder. Agonizing pain, the moment he'd saved her life.

She'd spent bleak months in a private psychiatric institution, where mental health experts tried to figure out why she'd tried to kill herself.

Really, it was simple. Shea had worshipped her big sister all her life. When Corey got braces, she wanted braces. When Corey was allowed to ride her bike alone, she wanted to ride her bike alone.

When Corey was gone, Shea wanted to be gone, too.

It took a long time and a lot of therapy for which her parents shelled out a massive amount of money before she changed her mind about that.

Recovering from a devastating loss doesn't protect you. It only arms you to face the other losses.

Shots . . . blood spatters . . . screams . . .

Her dying parents' screams, bystanders', and her own.

She survived, and she went on.

But if it happens again . . .

It won't. It can't. She'll never again lose someone she needs and depends on; someone who makes her feel safe and loved. Someone whose absence can leave a gaping hole.

There will never be another person in her life like that, because she won't let anyone in. She—

"Shea? Shea Daniels!"

She whirls at the sound of an unfamiliar voice.

A woman is standing by the storage shed, long hair whipping in the wind.

J.J.

"John is dead," Dr. Michaels had said the morning after J.J. had awakened to find her husband standing over the bed. "You couldn't have seen him."

"But he was there. He was so real."

"It's the medication. I'm going to adjust it again."

Had he? Had she thrown away the old medication and switched to the new? There are too many orange bottles to keep track of. Too many things to remember—among them, that John is dead.

Most of the time, she's aware of that. But Leila and Molly don't know, and so when she's with them, she pretends. It's nice to pretend. It makes everything feel so normal for a little while. It allows her to forget that John died on that horrible night just before Christmas, after J.J. had begun to follow Leila's advice, taking a sleeping pill and putting her phone on Do Not Disturb.

She did sleep better that first night, and the next. Then came record cold temperatures. A space heater ignited a five-alarm fire in a three-family house occupied by impoverished young families.

John became trapped trying to reach toddlers believed to be on the top floor. When they got him to the hospital, the doctors—and John—knew he couldn't survive his burns. He was conscious in the ICU, trying to hang on until she could get there. The hospital repeatedly tried to reach her, aware that he had only a few hours left, but her phone was silenced.

By the time she got the message and rushed to the hospital, he was gone. He'd died alone, asking for her.

Brian came, and they had a funeral, and all the firemen were there, and the mayor, and Brian's friends. So many people, so many strangers, hugging her and offering comforting platitudes that wouldn't change a damned thing. The people who lived on the top floor came to the funeral. They said he was a hero. They said that the toddlers had been staying with their grandparents that night. They weren't even there. It was for nothing. All for nothing

Telling Leila and Molly had never even occurred to J.J. She was in shock, consumed by grief. Brian handled everything—the arrangements, notifying people, every grim task associated with a loss of that magnitude.

"J.J. . . . just stay right where you are, okay?"

She blinks and looks back over her shoulder. The man approaching her isn't John because John is dead. And he isn't Brian because Brian is . . .

Brian is her rock. He helped her get through John's death.

But then he, too, vanished from her life, uniformed in the doorway that January day, tears streaming down his face.

"I'm sorry, Mom. Please. You have to understand. I made a commitment. My leave is over, and this is my job. I have to go on, and so do you. It's what Dad would want."

"No! He wouldn't want that! He wouldn't want you to just . . . just go off and risk your life, and . . . and . . ."

And leave me here alone.

But Brian—Brian, who was all she had left in the world, Brian, who knew she couldn't bear to lose anything else—Brian left. And then Brian died, too. Killed in action.

But now he's here again, and he's just a tiny baby who needs her.

"It's going to be okay, J.J.!" the man calls, inching closer. He's familiar, but she can't place him.

And the woman right behind him—she's beautiful, with flowing blond hair, wearing a pink nightgown. "Careful, J.J., honey. You're right at the edge."

She looks down and sees her toes aligned with the drop-off. And there's a baby in the carrier, and she's holding it so he must be her baby, but . . .

He doesn't look like Brian. Maybe the encroaching smoke is clouding her vision. Or maybe she's hallucinating again and there is no baby, no woman, no man, no drop-off. Because it's all so very strange, and it can't be right.

"Hey, J.J.?" The woman is right next to her now but she sounds as if she's coming from far away, or long ago.

She isn't real. This isn't really happening. The pills . . .
Dr. Michaels . . .

Deep breaths.

She inhales, and her lungs fill with smoke. The fires are
burning all around her, except in the sea.

"I need you to give me the baby, honey, okay? Thank you
so much for taking such good care of him."

"I'll help you. Here, let me take the carrier for you, J.J.,"
the man says.

He's right beside her, and he seems so real, and the
woman seems real and the baby and the cliff . . .

But no, that's wrong. The cliff isn't real, because when
she looks down, she sees that she's standing on a threadbare
mat. It's the one John had bought when she first moved into
his apartment "to fancy it up a little," he'd said.

Later, years later, they'd laughed about that. There's
nothing fancy about a patch of brown rug that reads "Welcome" in black block letters. Sometimes when they were
shopping at Walmart, he'd find a different mat—one that
was blue or green, or had scrolly script, or was etched with
flowers.

"Now, this is fancy," he'd say. "Let's get it."

But J.J. always said no. There was nothing better in the
world than setting foot on that worn brown mat and then
over the threshold. Nothing better than home, especially
when she's been away for so long, and John is there waiting
for her.

She steps forward, over the threshold.

SHEA

The woman is a stranger. Shea recognizes her from some-where, though she can't quite place her. She appears to be around Shea's age, dressed in jeans and hiking boots.

"I just need to talk to you for a few minutes."

On some level, Shea grasps the preposterousness—that this person she doesn't know, this person who shouldn't be here, thinks that Shea has a few minutes to talk when every second counts. When lives are hanging in the balance, and the baby is missing, and Leila is missing, and the fires are burning.

"Who are you?"

"Riley Robertson."

She pauses as if Shea should know the name. And she does, but . . .

"*Who* are you?"

"I'm a podcaster. And author," she adds, like an old ac-quaintance bragging in the supermarket aisle. "I host *Disappearing Acts*, and I'm writing a book about Chantal."

"You're the one who's been stalking Justin. I knew I should have gotten the damned restraining order."

"Restraining order? I haven't been stalking anyone. I'm just—"

"A podcaster. And an author. I heard. And you've been here . . . how long?"

"Just since yesterday."

"*Just* since yesterday? You've been here? On my property? In my house? In the cupola," she realizes, as the pieces fall into place. "That was you, snooping around, watching with binoculars."

"I didn't do anything wrong. I just—"

"You're trespassing! You're—"

"But It's not like I bothered anyone or stole anything. I'm just trying to figure out what happened to Chantal."

"Get out of here. Right now. Before I call the police."

"But I only want—"

"I don't care what you want, okay? I want you out of here."

"But—"

"There's an evacuation order! I'm leaving! We're all leaving. And if you don't, you'll *become* a *Disappearing Act* yourself, because this whole place is about to go up in flames, and . . ."

She swallows the rest, and the sorrow that swells in her throat at the thought of losing it. Without Windfall, what will she have? Nothing.

"An evacuation order? Is that real?"

"It's real."

"If I go, can I interview you some other time? About Chantal?"

"No."

"But I just want to know what happened to her, and why—"

"The entire world wants to know, okay? Including me. So if you ever find out, make sure to let me in on the secret," Shea says, and leaves her there.

She looks back over her shoulder a minute later to see Riley Robertson hurrying away toward the gate.

She'll never find Chantal. Even Shea doesn't know where she is now.

She only knows where she isn't. She knows—

A high, shrill sound shatters the night, and it isn't an echo from the past. It came from the cliff above the water. Shea breaks into a run.

J.J.

They say your whole life flashes before you at the very end, but that isn't true.

J.J. sees only Leila.

Leila, leading the way out this spot late last night, high above the sea, so that she could check her phone.

Leila, telling J.J. about her affair with Stef. She'd ended it because he told her he'd never leave his wife and children for her. Now she was hoping the money would change his mind.

Leila, who thought she knew everything and knew nothing at all.

"Money doesn't change a damned thing that matters," J.J. told her.

"It changes everything. We can have whatever we want. Do you realize we can buy houses like this, with views like this?"

"That's not what I want. Things like that don't matter to me."

"What? Are you crazy?"

"No! I'm not crazy! Don't say I'm crazy!"

"I didn't mean—"

"And don't say that the money is going to change everything, because for me, it's not going to change anything."

"What are you talking about, J.J.? Of course it will. You're still in shock."

"I'm not in shock."

"Yes, you are. You feel like it isn't real, but you're wrong."

Leila, telling J.J. how she feels. That she's wrong.

J.J. reached into her pocket and pulled out a cigarette and a lighter.

Leila reached into her pocket and pulled out . . .

Was it the lottery ticket? She was supposed to put it in the bank! She'd said it's not safe in fire season; that the wind can shift and you can lose everything . . .

"See this? We're the September Girls. You, me, and Molly. Together forever."

J.J. said nothing, putting the cigarette between her lips and holding the lighter to it.

"Ooh, can I have a drag?" Leila reached for the cigarette, still holding the ticket. The lighter's flame caught the edge and ignited it.

"What the hell are you doing?"

"Blow it out! Just blow it out!" J.J. shouted.

Leila tried, but it was burning in her hand, burning her hand. She screamed in pain and let go. The wind caught it and carried it. Leila tried to grab it, but it was beyond her reach. She leapt into the air, one last attempt, but it was borne like a flaming arrow into the sea.

Leila came down hard, lost her balance, and went over in a hailstorm of dirt and pebbles.

J.J. screamed for her, and looked for her, and there was nothing but jagged rocks and foaming surf.

The next thing she knew, she was in bed, trying not to think about John or burning canyons, or burning tickets and Leila . . .

But that couldn't have happened. There was a pill bottle on the seat beside her, and she knew she must have taken her medication and it had caused her to hallucinate again, just like the time she thought John was standing over her bed.

John is dead.

Leila . . .

Leila, too, is dead.

Leila fell into the sea and the ticket went up in flames.

It might have happened like that—the ticket catching fire, Leila falling over the edge. . . .

Or Leila might have told her about the affair with Stef, and J.J. might have snatched the delicate gold chain from Leila's neck—the one with the sapphire pendant that was supposed to remind them all of how much they meant to each other. The one she'd forgotten to even pack, and then claimed had been stolen from her room.

J.J. might have thrown Leila's pendant into the sea. Or maybe Leila hadn't been wearing it at all.

She might have snatched the ticket from Leila's hand and held it to her lighter and lit it on fire. Or maybe she hadn't had the ticket at all. Maybe it had been a photo strip from last weekend in Vegas, when the three of them had crammed into one of those booths together and posed, arm in arm, making silly faces. September Girls.

Maybe J.J. had set it on fire, Leila had lunged for it and fallen.

Or J.J. might have pushed her, hard, because Leila had told her about Stef and Leila had been so smug and Leila had made her turn off her phone that December night and John had died alone and it was Leila's fault, and J.J. hates her for it, and maybe she'd wanted her to die and maybe she hadn't, and maybe she wants to die and maybe she doesn't, and it doesn't matter because it's going to happen and it's happening and—

MOLLY

"Noooooo!" Molly screeches as J.J. walks off the cliff as though she's stepping into an elevator. "Noooooooo!"

As she topples forward, J.J.'s hand releases the baby's carrier. It lands in the spot where she'd been standing a split second before she disappeared over the edge.

Dawson wails and flails and the seat rocks violently forward, back, forward, back . . .

Molly catches the handle and pulls. She falls backward with the seat on top of her. She hears Dawson sobbing and she knows that he's safe. She has her son, and for a long, long time, nothing else matters, and J.J.'s words echo in her head as if she'd spoken to them just now.

Don't ever let anything happen to your son. You have to protect him. Keep him close to you, always.

Molly comforts her child, holding him close until his sobs subside. But someone else is still crying.

Shea.

Shea, wrapped in Beck's arms, face buried in his shoulder.

"Is J.J . . . ?" Molly asks, looking again to the spot where she'd last seen her friend.

Beck meets her gaze with a somber shake of his head.

Hi, guys, welcome to *Disappearing Acts*. I'm host Riley Robertson, former investigative reporter, current podcaster, and perennial snoop!

This is our final episode of *Whatever Happened to Chantal Charbonneau?* Today, we're going to examine leads and sightings over the last twenty years that might back up my conclusion that Chantal is still alive. We're also going to interview several experts who knew her, and who have evidence that strongly supports the theory that she staged her disappearance.

First up is renowned plastic surgeon Sara Bajwa, with whom Chantal had a consultation about facial cosmetic surgery early in 2001.

We'll also talk to Amber Mitchell, a former investment assistant who says that Chantal transferred large amounts of money to offshore accounts in preparation, enough to fund her disappearance and allow her to live the rest of her life in comfort, if not extravagance.

Finally, we'll talk to my friend and colleague Jackson Borden, author of the bestseller *Presumed Dead*, about real-life cases involving people who have staged their deaths, and how and why they might do it.

Because let's face it. We've all thought about it, haven't we? What it would be like to walk away from our lives and get a do-over?

I think that's exactly what Chantal Charbonneau did, and I think that at the end of this podcast, you're going to agree.

MONDAY MORNING

SHEA

In the wee hours, Shea learned that the barricades had been removed from the stretch of highway leading to Windfall. Fires are still burning north and east of here, and the area remains shrouded in smoke, but the Santa Anas are dying down and there's rain in the forecast.

By 4 a.m., Shea has dropped the dogs with Justin and is in the car, driving past hillsides reduced to cinders and smoldering ruins where homes once stood. She doesn't know what, if anything, is left of her home, but she's prepared for the worst.

She'd evacuated just before midnight Saturday, after Molly, devastated when she grasped what had happened, had been taken away in an ambulance with Dawson. Protocol, given the circumstances. Both are going to be just fine; the medics had assured Shea.

But they couldn't save J.J. Deputies and investigators and rescue units had searched in vain for the woman who'd jumped to her death. They found no trace of her. The sea had swallowed her and swept her away.

It's what Chantal had wanted everyone to believe had happened to her.

Corey was the one who told her that.

"She just couldn't take it anymore," she'd told Shea on another grim September day, so long ago. "That's what she told Daddy."

"How do you know?"

"I heard them talking. About how they're going to make it look like she died, because that's the only way she can get away. She said she can't live like this anymore. She said she feels like a bird in a cage. She just wants to be free. I get that, don't you?"

Shea didn't get it then. The bird, or Chantal, or Corey . . .

How you can possess all the things so many people believe make life worth living—wealth, success, beauty, health—and still feel trapped in a meaningless existence.

But later, long after they were gone, and her parents were gone, she understood—far more than Corey ever had. She found the truth among her father's papers.

Chantal wasn't just her parents' employer, or Corey and Shea's benefactor.

She was Daddy's younger sister. And she was Corey's mother.

Her real name was Susie Daniels. She'd never lived in France, or Louisiana. She'd grown up in some godforsaken Rust Belt town Daddy never liked to talk about, in a deeply religious household. When she got pregnant as a teenager, her parents disowned her.

Daddy was married by then, living in another city. He

and Mom took in Susie and kept her child to raise as their own. There was no legal adoption, only an agreement signed by all three, promising never to divulge the truth. There was a letter, too, in loopy teenage handwriting—Susie promising her brother and sister-in-law that when she became a star, she would pay for her daughter's support and reimburse them for everything they'd done for her.

She really did take a bus to Hollywood—that part of the story was true—where she reinvented herself and her life story.

She kept her promise to her family, moving them to California and into her home under the guise of hiring domestic staff.

Shea wonders sometimes whether Chantal ever comprehended what she'd given up for stardom, the dream she held dearest, the dream that had come true. She wonders whether, in the end, Chantal realized she'd made a mistake. Whether she'd abandoned the life she had because she wanted to chase another dream, or whether she could simply no longer face seeing Corey every day, wondering whether she'd made the right choice, the right sacrifice.

"Daddy told her she can come home if she changes her mind," Corey had told Shea after Chantal vanished. "He said Windfall will always be waiting for her, and so will we."

In the end, only Shea was left to wait, though she knows now that Chantal is never coming back. If she was going to, she would have after Corey died, or after Shea's parents had. Maybe she didn't know about those losses.

Maybe there was no room in her new life for a lost soul who'd lost everything. Or maybe she, too, had died.

It doesn't matter, does it?

Not anymore.

Shea yawns, sucking in air so heavily scented with wildfire that she turns toward the distant canyons, expecting to see smoke and flames edging closer. They aren't.

A hand comes to rest on her shoulder and she remembers that she isn't alone. Beck is here, behind the wheel, has been beside her throughout the ordeal.

"It's late," he says.

She shakes her head and gestures at the dashboard clock. "It's early."

"You should get some sleep."

"So should you."

"I have to meet Warren McGovern at the bank in the Valley as soon as it opens."

"The ticket isn't going to be in that safe-deposit box," she says.

Leila obviously wanted to throw off suspicion, already planning her escape.

"I'm aware. I still have to go through the motions. They're sending a couple of detectives."

Right. It's part of the missing person investigation. Before the evacuation, law enforcement had combed the house and grounds for clues, and they'd taken Leila's belongings as evidence, but she's gone.

She'll eventually have to claim the money. By then,

though, her identity and whereabouts will be shrouded in mystery. Shea knows how that works. It's what she does.

She still has so many questions about Leila. She's left behind a trail of shattered lives, including her children's. But money, that much money, can make you forget who you really are, and what matters in life. Nobody knows that better than Shea.

"Are you ready?" Beck asks, as they round the last bend.

"No."

"Do you want me to pull over so that you can—"

"No," she says again. "I'll never be ready, but like you said, it's time to move on."

"When did I say that?"

"Maybe I just thought you did. You do like to tell me what to do," she adds, to lighten the moment.

He smiles. "I told you, I'm working on that."

"Appreciated." She takes a deep breath. "And I didn't tell you, but I'm working on being more open and, you know . . . sharing."

"You don't have to talk about the past, Shea. Not with me."

"But I do. Not right now, but . . ." She takes another deep breath, watching the road. "I can't keep it all locked away from you, or . . . or even from me. I can't keep running. Not unless I want to be alone for the rest of my life. I thought I did, because when you let people in, there's so much more to lose, and I've never been willing to risk it, but . . ."

She shakes her head. This is so much harder than she'd expected.

She closes her eyes, and she hears her voice, a little-girl voice. *It's too scary!*

And Corey's voice, too. *You're strong and brave.*

And then Beck's, here and now, not talking about cobwebs or spiderwebs. "Shea? You said *but* . . . ?"

"But now I'm not sure. About taking that risk. It's scary, you know?"

"I know," he says quietly.

Then they're at the gate, and he pulls to a stop alongside the electronic keypad. She takes it all in—the cascading scarlet bougainvillea, and the iron nameplate on the stone gatepost.

Windfall.

Beck enters the code and the gate glides open. As they drive toward the house, he steers with one hand and reaches over with the other to squeeze hers.

"Do you think it's gone?" she asks, at the last second.

"It might be."

But it isn't. There it stands, isolated in the clearing, tall and imposing as a monument.

That's what it is in so many ways, bearing testament to a traumatic time in Shea's own life and so many others'.

Maybe there's a part of her that had been hoping it had burned to the ground. Then there would be no decision to make about moving on and letting go.

Staring at the cupola, she sees a shadow against the

window and is certain that it's a person—the podcaster, or a ghost, or Chantal, back at last.

But she's wrong. It's just a fat gull, perched on the parapet.

With a fluttering of wings, it lifts off and soars into the smoky sky.

MOLLY

Molly stares out the limousine window, one hand resting on Dawson's arm as he dozes beside her. The medical staff had checked him over thoroughly, and Molly, too. Not a scratch on the baby, thank goodness. Molly's bruised and sore from her fall after wrenching her son to safety, but she'll heal. Physically, anyway.

It's going to be a long time before she stops seeing J.J.'s wildly troubled, vacant eyes every time she closes her own.

Now they're heading to the airport. No red-eye or connecting flights this time. It's a private plane.

"But I can't pay for that," Molly had told Shea yesterday, back at the fancy hotel where she and Dawson had gone after the hospital.

"I can."

"You're already paying for the hotel. I can't let you—"

"You're my client, Molly. I have to get you and Dawson home safely."

"But I'm not a client anymore. Leila was, and she's . . ."

Gone. Leila is gone with the ticket and the money that was going to change Molly's life, and J.J.'s, too. Maybe that's why she'd taken her own life. Maybe, for all J.J.'s talk about money not mattering, she had felt like it was all she had left after John's death.

Molly wants to believe they're together again. That J.J. is in a better place with the love of her life.

And she wants to believe that she, Molly, can turn her own life around. She can start by telling the truth about her pregnancy. Not just to her family.

She has to tell Ross, who will be relieved at being off the hook financially and paternally.

And Stef, for whom Molly is pretty sure this will change nothing.

And one day, she'll tell Dawson. Years from now, when she's raised him to be a strong, wonderful, understanding human being. When he's old enough to grasp that good people sometimes make bad choices. Even people you love. And that adulthood is about taking responsibility for bad decisions as well as celebrating the good ones.

Her phone buzzes, and she reaches into her pocket. It has to be her mother. She's been calling and texting ever since Molly reached out from the hospital to let her know what had happened. In a few hours, she and Dad will meet Molly and Dawson at the Savannah airport.

Pulling out her phone, though, she sees that the call is from Shea.

"Hello?"

"Molly! Are you on your way to the airport?"

"Yes. Thank you again for arranging this. Did you find out anything about the house?"

"Still standing. In fact, I'm there right now, and I know you're anxious to get home, but . . . you might want to come back here instead."

"Back to Windfall? I thought you were going to have our stuff shipped to Savannah?"

"Oh, I am."

"Then why do you want me to come back?" Molly asks, thinking that nothing in the world is important enough to draw her back to that cursed mansion.

"Beck went to the bank with Leila's ex-husband."

"Right. To check the safe-deposit box."

"Yes. And, Molly . . . the lottery ticket was there after all."

She gasps. "What? Are you sure?"

"I'm looking at it right now. Here, I'll read off the numbers. Let's see. The first one is 9 . . ."

Yes. 9, signifying September, the birth month they'd shared.

"Then 12 . . ."

September 12. Leila's birthday.

"16 . . ."

September 16. J.J.'s birthday.

"29."

September 29, Molly's birthday.

"40 . . ."

Yes. Their age. The milestone they'd celebrated together just last weekend.

"And the last one . . ."

"46." Molly says it with her.

She closes her eyes to blink away the tears and she sees that the three of them buying those September birthstone necklaces, wearing them, promising to wear them forever.

September Girls.

"So Leila didn't . . . she didn't . . ."

"She didn't," Shea tells her, but there's a note of sorrow in her voice.

Molly wants to ask what she knows, and where Leila is, but she can't. Not yet. Not now.

"So how about coming back, Molly?" Shea asks. "We can get the paperwork going on this. It's going to be complicated."

"I know." Molly nods and looks down at Dawson. "And we will, but right now . . . I have to go home, Shea. I just have to go home. My parents are waiting, and my sisters, and . . . I just really need to see them, and hug them. I hope you understand."

"I do," Shea says. "More than you can imagine. The money can wait, Molly. Go hug your family."

EIGHT MONTHS LATER

Hi, guys, welcome to *Disappearing Acts*. I'm host Riley Robertson, former investigative reporter, current podcaster, perennial snoop . . . and bestselling author!

That's right, my book, *Chameleon: Whatever Happened to Chantal Charbonneau?*, hit the shelves last week, and debuted at number nine on the *New York Times* Nonfiction Bestseller List!

Fans of my book and this podcast are aware that Windfall, the site of Hollywood's most mysterious disappearance, is reportedly cursed. But for one unfortunate listener, a visit to the mansion ended with history repeating itself.

Today, we'll return to that familiar setting and meet a whole new set of characters as we kick off a brand-new season: *Whatever Happened to Leila Randolph?*

More from

Wendy Corsi Staub

The Other Family

The Butcher's Daughter

Dead Silence

Little Girl Lost

Bone White

Blue Moon

Blood Red

The Black Widow

The Perfect Stranger

The Good Sister

Shadowkiller

Sleepwalker

Nightwatcher

Hell to Pay

Scared to Death

Live to Tell